TRIPLE THE FUN

BY
MAUREEN CHILD

Published in Great Britain 2015
by Mills & Boon, an imprint of Harlequin (UK) Limited,
Eton House, 18-24 Paradise Road, Richmond, Surrey, TW9 1SR

© 2015 Maureen Child

ISBN: 978-0-263-25260-6

51-0515

Harlequin (UK) Limited's policy is to use papers that are natural, renewable and recyclable products and made from wood grown in sustainable forests. The logging and manufacturing processes conform to the legal environmental regulations of the country of origin.

Printed and bound in Spain
by CPI, Barcelona

Maureen Child writes for the Mills & Boon® Desire™ line and can't imagine a better job. A seven-time finalist for the prestigious Romance Writers of America RITA® Award, Maureen is the author of more than one hundred romance novels. Her books regularly appear on bestseller lists and have won several awards, including a Prism Award, a National Readers' Choice Award, a Colorado Romance Writers Award of Excellence and a Golden Quill Award.

One of her books, *The Soul Collector*, was made into a CBS TV movie starring Melissa Gilbert, Bruce Greenwood and Ossie Davis. If you look closely, in the last five minutes of the movie you'll spot Maureen, who was an extra in the last scene.

Maureen believes that laughter goes hand in hand with love, so her stories are always filled with humor. The many letters she receives assure her that her readers love to laugh as much as she does. Maureen Child is a native Californian but has recently moved to the mountains of Utah.

For all of you reading this book right now!
Because of you I'm able to tell the stories I want
to tell. I'm incredibly grateful for each of you!

One

"You're *where*?" Connor King didn't bother to hide the laughter in his voice. He kicked back in his office chair, propped his feet on the edge of his desk and stared out the window at his view of the Pacific Ocean. Holding the phone to his left ear, he listened to his twin's grumbling with a widening smile on his face.

"With the twins at the park near the house."

"How the mighty have crashed and burned," Connor chortled, shaking his head. Only two years ago, his identical twin, Colton, had been single, driven, a wild man who chased down every extreme adventure their company offered to other risk takers around the world.

Then Colton had found out that his ex-wife, Penny, had given birth to twins, a boy and a girl. His world had been thrown into turmoil and he'd been forced to make some real changes and face some hard truths. Though he'd nearly blown the whole thing, Colt had wised up in time to build a new life. Now he had a wife and two kids and was happier than ever before.

That didn't mean that Connor wouldn't give him grief at every opportunity, though.

"A *playdate*," he repeated with a laugh. "Man…"

"Yeah, yeah," Colt muttered. "Have your laugh and get it over with. Then we can talk about the Ireland plans. You still flying over there to check things out?"

"That's the idea," Connor said, still chuckling. In the last year, King Extreme Adventures had morphed into King Family Adventures. When Colt had finally realized what was most important in his life, he and Connor had reevaluated their business plan. Extreme adventures were risky and dangerous, and the potential client base very limited. On the other hand, by switching the emphasis of their company to family adventures, they'd opened themselves up to a worldwide audience.

Sure, they still ran the extreme adventures for those that wanted it, but since shifting their business focus, the company had grown exponentially.

"I'll be staying at Ashford Castle and Jefferson's setting me up with a guide to show me around the area."

"Amazing," Colt muttered. "We go from offering black diamond ski runs in the Alps to family tours of Ireland."

"Things change," Connor reminded him. "You should know that better than anyone."

"Not complaining," his twin said, then in a louder voice called out, "Reid, don't throw sand at your sister."

Con chuckled. "Riley can take care of herself."

"Yeah—there she goes. Sand right back at him." Colt laughed a little. "Penny's at home painting their bedroom.

I figured taking the dangerous duo to the park was the easier job. Should've known better."

While his brother talked, Connor looked up as their admin, Linda, walked into his office with the mail. She smiled at him, handed the stack of letters over and left the office. Idly, Con picked out a legal-size manila envelope from the rest and threw the others on his desk. Catching the phone between his ear and his shoulder, he ripped open the flap, pulled out the papers and skimmed them. It only took a second for him to say, "What the hell?"

Colt paused, then asked, "What's wrong?"

"You're not going to believe this," Con muttered, straightening in his desk chair, staring at the papers in his hand. The edges of his vision darkened until he was looking at the typeset words as if through a telescope. Despite the legal language designed to make most people feel inadequate to the task of deciphering it, Connor understood enough to know that his world had just taken a major shift.

"What's going on?"

Colt's voice in his ear sounded far away, as though the phone had become a tunnel miles long. Connor's gaze locked on the phrase that had leaped out at him. A heavy band tightened around his chest until drawing a breath seemed a Herculean feat. A ball of ice dropped into the pit of his stomach.

He swallowed hard and made himself say the words. "Apparently, I'm a *father*."

An hour later, Con was standing on the flagstone patio at Colt's cliff-side home in Dana Point. Staring out at the ocean below them, Con hardly noticed the sailboats, the surfers or the waves pounding against the shore with a regular rhythm that sounded like a heartbeat. If he turned his head to the left, he'd be able to see his own house, not a mile farther down the cliff road.

Colt's house was modern, with lots of glass and chrome, though Penny had made inroads there, infusing the place with warmth and color over the last couple of years. Con's place was more traditional, though it clung to the face of the cliff as well.

But he wasn't thinking about houses, style or the damn sea that relentlessly swept in and out. All he could think was: *triplets*. He'd outdone his brother by one, though he couldn't really take credit for it, could he? Sure, it had been his sperm, but it wasn't as though he'd been involved any further than that.

Hell. He hadn't even known the babies existed until today. Because a woman he'd trusted—a *friend*—had lied to him. And that was almost harder to believe than the fact that he was suddenly the father of three.

He had to get to the bottom of this. Find out everything he could before deciding on a plan of action. But there *would* be a plan. He was sure of that much, at least. What exactly it would entail was still a mystery.

Connor had put the King family lawyers on the case before he left to come to Colt and Penny's house. He was going to be logical. Rational. He wasn't giving in to his instinct to *do* something. Anything. But it wasn't easy.

So far, all he knew was the name of the woman currently suing him for child support. Dina Cortez. Sister of Elena Cortez, wife of Jackie Francis.

Jackie.

Shaking his head, Con gritted his teeth against a wild rush of anger. Jackie had been Con's best friend all through high school and college. When he got burned in love, Jackie was the one he turned to. She was the one woman in his life he'd always trusted—mainly because she'd never wanted anything from him. In fact, the only time they'd ever argued was second year of college when they'd both fallen for the same girl. A faint smile briefly twisted his mouth as he remembered that rather than discover which of them the woman might go for, they'd both chosen their friendship over the redhead.

Three years ago, Con had been Jackie's best man when she married her longtime girlfriend, Elena Cortez. Hell, he'd even taken her to Vegas for a mini bachelorette party before the wedding. He would have bet the King family fortune that Jackie would never lie to him. And yet…

"So stupid," he muttered, stabbing his fingers through his hair as a cold June wind pushed at him.

"How were you supposed to know?" Penny King stepped up alongside him and gave his arm a pat.

As much as he appreciated the support from his sister-in-law, she simply couldn't understand the level of betrayal he was feeling. *He* could hardly grasp it. "I should have checked. When Jackie moved to Northern California, I should have kept in touch. Maybe then…"

"None of this is your fault," Colt said as he walked up beside his wife and stood staring at his twin.

"My sperm. My babies. My fault." Con shook his head and tightened his grip on the bottle of beer he didn't even want. He knew his family was on his side, but the bottom line here was, he hadn't made a move to keep up with Jackie. He'd merely let her slide out of his life. If he'd done things differently, he wouldn't be in a state of shock today.

"You know," Colt murmured sagely, "it's easy to see

where you made a wrong turn when you look back at the road you're on. Not so easy when you're looking ahead."

Frowning, Connor grumbled, "You can spin this any way you want. Fact is, I screwed up."

And nothing his family said could change that. Turning his face back into the wind, gaze fixed on the frothing ocean, memories rose up and nearly choked him.

"Connor, we want to have a baby."

He laughed, dropped one arm around Jackie's shoulder and said, "Congratulations! So it's a trip to the sperm bank for you guys! See? I always told you that you'd need a man eventually."

Jackie grinned and shook her head. "Funny guy."

"I try. Which one of you's getting pregnant?"

She leaned into him and shrugged. "Elena's going to do the heavy lifting. I'm her support system."

"You'll be great parents," he assured her and steered her toward the bar in the corner of his living room. Once there, he dug a couple of beers out of the minifridge and opened them. Handing one to Jackie, he tapped the neck of his bottle against hers. Then, frowning a little, he asked, "How does that work, though? What does the kid call you? Are you both Mommy? Mommy One and Mommy Two?"

"Yeah, I don't know. We'll figure that out when we get there." Jackie took a sip of her beer and said, "There's a lot to take care of before we get to the kid talking. And part of that is, Elena and I, we wanted to ask you something important."

"Okay..." Connor picked up on her sudden nervousness, and it was so unlike Jackie, he was concerned. "What's going on?"

Rather than answer right away, she took another sip

*of beer, chewed at her bottom lip and then blew out a
long breath. "See, this is why Elena will carry the baby.
I don't think I could give up beer for nine months."*

*"Uh-huh," Connor said with a frown. "Quit stalling.
What is it you're trying to say?"*

*They'd spent the day together, catching a movie, going
to check out the Porsche Connor was thinking of buying
and ending up back at his house for a quick one-on-one
game of basketball. She hadn't said a word about any
of this. Suddenly, though, she wasn't being herself, and
that was starting to worry him.*

*"Okay," she repeated, then took a deep breath. Lift-
ing her gaze to his, she said, "The thing is, Elena and I
have been talking about this for a long time."*

*"Yeah? Not surprising. You're both all about hearth
and home—"*

*She snorted. "Yeah, we're practically a '50's sitcom.
Anyway, you know how you just said we'd have to head
for the sperm bank because, you know, obviously we need
a donor, and—" She paused for another sip of beer as
if her throat was too dry for her to force the words out.
"Okay, I'm just gonna put it out there. We don't want to
go with some stranger we picked out of a catalog. We'd
like you to be the baby daddy."*

*Surprise slapped at him. For a second or two, he
could only stare at his best friend. Jackie's gaze was sure
and steady, but there was also a flicker of understanding
there, too, as if she knew exactly what he was feeling.
Well, hell. He hadn't really thought about who might be
the father of the child his friend wanted so badly—he'd
assumed that she and Elena would go to a sperm bank
and pick out some genius donor.*

But now that she'd asked him, Connor realized it

made sense. He and Jackie were practically family. Who the hell else would she ask?

"Elena wants this, too?"

"Completely," Jackie assured him, and now that everything was out in the open, she was clearly more relaxed. "Con, there's no pressure on you, okay? Feel free to say no, with no hard feelings between us, I swear. Just...don't say no right away. Think about it, all right?"

Connor reached out, grabbed her and pulled her in for a tight hug. She sighed, wrapped her arms around his middle and held on. "I know this is big, Con. Seriously big. And I know it's kind of weird, me asking you for your baby stuff. But—" she tipped her head back and looked at him "—we really want this and we want that... connection to the baby's father, you know? You mean a lot to us. Not just me."

He gave her a squeeze. "Yeah, I know. I love you, too."

"God, we're mushy all of a sudden."

"Babies'll do that to you, I hear," Con said.

Her eyes went misty. "A baby. Hard to imagine me a mom."

"No, it's not," he assured her. And seeing that dreamy, wistful look on her face would have decided him even if he hadn't already made the choice. They'd been friends so long, how could he not help her when she needed it? "I'd have a condition, Jack..."

She sucked in a breath and held it. "What?"

"I can't just father a kid and walk away. I'll have to be a part of my child's life."

Part-time father, *he told himself.* All of the fun and little of the hassles.

"Absolutely, Con. Agreed."

"All right then." Connor swung her in a circle and Jackie shrieked with laughter. When he set her on her feet again, he gave her a fast, hard kiss and said, "Let's make a baby."

They'd tried.

But Jackie told him the insemination hadn't taken. When he'd offered to help them try again, she'd turned him down. Said that she and Elena were moving to Northern California to get a fresh start. Then she'd sort of disappeared from his life. No phone calls. No nothing.

He'd allowed it to happen, too, so he couldn't throw all the blame on Jackie for that. "I should have checked," he said again, hating that he hadn't.

"Yeah, well—" Colt leaned back against the low stone wall separating the patio from a wide swath of manicured lawn "—who would have expected Jackie to lie to you?"

That was the hardest part to swallow, Connor admitted silently. He'd always trusted her. Had never doubted what she told him. And all this time, she'd hidden *his children* from him.

Con shook his head and squinted into the wind. His heartbeat raced and the ice in his stomach was colder, deeper somehow than it had been only an hour before. And after all the lies, he couldn't even yell at her. Because she and Elena were dead. He hadn't been able to cut through most of the legalese in the damn letter from the lawyer, but that much he'd caught. Dina Cortez, the babies' guardian, named by the *late* Jackie and Elena Francis, was the one suing him.

How the hell could he mourn his friend when he was so furious with her all he wanted to do was rage at her for what she'd done?

"So who's Dina Cortez?" Colt folded his arms over his chest.

"Elena's sister," Connor told him. "I met her at the wedding. She was Elena's maid of honor and the only one of her family who showed up." He frowned. He still couldn't understand how family didn't support family, no matter what. "Don't remember much about her, really."

"Doesn't matter, I guess," Colt mused. "You'll be getting to know her pretty damn well soon enough."

"True." And he'd have plenty to say once he met up with Dina Cortez again.

"Sure," Dina said into the phone. "We can cater your anniversary party on the twenty-fourth. No problem. If it's all right with you, we can meet later this week to discuss the menu."

Idly tapping her pen against the desktop calendar already filled with doodles, squiggles and notes incomprehensible to anyone but her, Dina listened to her latest client talk with only half an ear.

How could she concentrate when she knew that very soon, she was going to be clashing with one of the Kings of California? Connor King, father of the triplets even now playing on the floor beside her, was a member of a family with more money than God and far more power than she could ever hope to claim.

She'd met him once before, when Dina's sister, Elena, had married her longtime partner, Jackie Francis. Connor had been Jackie's best man and he'd caught Dina's attention from the moment she saw him. Of course, any woman would have been captivated by the man. He was gorgeous and possessed that innate sense of being in charge that was both alluring and irritating to a strong woman.

His easy relationship with Jackie was one of long standing; they'd been best friends since high school. But what was more impressive to Dina at the time was that he had been so focused on being there for his friend. Most single guys used a wedding as an opportunity to pick up women. But Connor hadn't paid attention to anyone but his friend.

Of course, he might be feeling a little differently toward Jackie at the moment. What Jackie and Elena had done to him was unforgivable.

While her client rambled on in her ear, Dina shifted her gaze to the babies behind a series of child gates. When the kids came to live with her, she had cordoned off a section of her work area in the kitchen. Blankets were piled on the floor, toys were scattered everywhere and three beautiful thirteen-month-old babies giggled and squealed and babbled to each other in a language no one but the three of them could possibly understand.

In a few short months, those babies had become Dina's whole world and it terrified her to think of what Connor King might do when he found out about them. Would he fight her for custody? Oh, boy, she hoped not. There was no way she could win in a legal battle with a King.

Her client finally wound down and in the sudden silence, Dina said quickly, "Right. I'll give you a call in a day or two and we'll set up that meeting. Okay, great. Thank you for calling. Goodbye."

She hung up and her fingers rested lightly on the back of the receiver. Naturally, as soon as she was off the phone, the babies got quiet. Smiling, she looked at them, two boys and a girl, and felt a hard, swift tug at her heart. She loved her niece and nephews, but being a single mother wasn't something she had planned for.

But then, Jackie and Elena hadn't *planned* to die, had they? Tears stung the backs of her eyes and she blinked them away. She looked at those shining, smiling faces watching her, and Dina felt such sorrow for her sister. She and Elena had been close, joined together against the chaos their mother had created. With their grandmother, the two sisters had formed a unit that had been shattered when Elena died.

Heart aching, Dina thought about her big sister and wished desperately that things were different. Elena had wanted nothing more, for most of her life, than to be a mother. She'd dreamed of having her own family.

Then she and her wife, Jackie, had finally succeeded in having the children that completed them, only to die before their triplets were a year old. The unfairness of it ripped at Dina and lodged a hard knot of pain in the center of her chest. But crying wouldn't help. She should know. Dina had cried an ocean of tears in the first couple of weeks after her sister and her wife died unexpectedly. So she was done with tears, but not panic.

Panic wasn't going anywhere. It came to haunt her in the middle of the night when she lay awake trying to figure out how to care for three babies all on her own. It walked beside her when she took the kids for a walk in their triple stroller. It whispered in her ear every time she bid on a catering job and didn't get it.

Which was one of the reasons she had decided to sue Connor King. He had money. Besides, he had been a big part of Jackie and Elena's lives. He had been prepared to be a part of the kids' lives. He owed it to his children to help pay for their support. With fewer financial worries, she could hire a part-time nanny to assist her in taking care of the triplets. Not that she was looking to bail out of caring for them—she wasn't. But she had to work and leaving them with a babysitter—even a great one like Jamie, the teenage girl who lived next door—just wasn't a permanent solution.

Sadie, Sage and Sam were all looking to her for protection. For safety. For love. She wouldn't fail them. Smiling down as the boys wrestled and Sadie slapped her teddy bear, Dina promised, "You'll know who your mommies were, sweet babies. I'll make sure of it. They loved you so much."

Sadie chewed on her bear's ear and Dina huffed out a sigh. Raising three babies alone wouldn't be easy, but she would do it. The triplets were what was important now, and Dina would do whatever she had to do to protect them. And on that thought, she stood up and announced, "You guys ready for a treat?"

Three heads spun toward her with identical expressions of eager anticipation. She laughed a little as Sadie pulled herself to her feet and demanded, "Up!"

"After your snack, okay, sweet girl?" The sweet girl in question's bottom lip quivered and Dina had to steel her heart against giving in. If she got Sadie up, then Sage and Sam would want out, too, and instead of a snack, she'd spend the next half hour chasing the three of them through her house. And, since it was closing in on their bedtime, she didn't want them getting all worked up anyway.

Before any of them could start complaining—*loudly*—Dina hustled to the counter to slice up a couple of bananas and pour milk into three sippy cups. Thank heaven Elena and Jackie had weaned them off bottles early. As soon as the kids were settled, gnawing happily on bananas and laughing together, the doorbell rang.

"You guys be good," she said and headed down the hall to the front door. She took a quick peek out the side window at the man on her porch and gasped. *Connor King*. The image of him was so clear and sharp in her memory, it was almost weird to see him standing on her porch.

Panic swam through her veins and she wasn't even surprised. She was becoming used to that out-of-control sensation, and she was pretty sure that wasn't a good thing. Somehow, Dina hadn't expected this meeting to happen so quickly. Maybe she should have. He was a King and he'd just found out he was the father of three children. Of course he would show up. Of course he would start pushing his metaphorical weight around. She knew enough about him and his family to know that he was going to be a formidable opponent, no matter what.

And since there was no ignoring him, she squared her shoulders, lifted her chin and yanked the door open. "Connor King," she said. "I wasn't expecting you."

"You should have been," he ground out tightly, then pushed past her into the house. "Where are my kids?"

Two

Conner had come for his kids, but now couldn't take his eyes off the woman who'd opened the door. Lust surged through him, grabbed him at the base of his throat and held on tight. All he could do was try to breathe through it.

The woman currently glaring at him had huge, chocolate-brown eyes, thick black hair hanging loose around her shoulders and long, gorgeous legs displayed by the white shorts she wore. Her short-sleeved red T-shirt clung to her body, showing off breasts that were just the right size to fill a man's hands.

Con couldn't understand how he hadn't noticed her at Jackie and Elena's wedding two years ago. Or how he'd managed to forget her. This was *not* a forgettable woman.

"Dina Cortez?" he asked, though he knew damn well who she was.

"Yes. And you're Connor King."

He nodded. Lust was still there, clawing at him, but he breathed through it and got back on track. "Now that the formalities are over, where are the kids?"

She folded her arms beneath her breasts, lifted her chin and said, "You shouldn't be here."

"Yeah," Con told her. "That's what my lawyer said, too."

In fact, he hadn't needed his lawyer to tell him to stay clear until they had more answers. Con knew he shouldn't have come, but there was no way he could stay away, either. He was a father. Of triplets. How the hell was a man supposed to ignore that?

He'd had to come, see the kids and find out what he could for himself, minus lawyerspeak. His twin had understood, though Penny had argued against it. But then, a couple of years ago, Colt had barged right in, too, to get a look at his twins and to confront the woman who'd given birth to them and then kept them a secret.

Well, Con couldn't face down Jackie or Elena, but the triplets were here, which explained, at least to him, why he was.

"Lawyers can still do their legal dance," he said, silently congratulating himself on keeping the temper still frothing inside him at a low boil. "For now, I had to come."

"Why?"

"*Why?*" He choked out a short laugh and shook his head. "Because I just found out I'm a father by hearing that I'm being sued for child support."

"Maybe if you had kept in contact with Jackie and Elena you would have known earlier," she pointed out.

"Seriously? You really want to go there? Maybe if

my best friend hadn't *lied* to me about those kids, this wouldn't be an issue," he argued and took a step closer. "And your *sister* was in on those lies," he reminded her tightly.

She blew out a breath and seemed to release some of the anger he could still see churning in her eyes. "Fine. You're right. They didn't tell me, either, you know. About you, I mean. They didn't tell me who the babies' father was."

His breath exploded in a rush. He was angry and had nowhere to focus it. He and Dina had been caught up in a web spun by Jackie and Elena. God, he wanted five minutes with Jackie just to demand some answers. But since he wasn't going to get that time, he said, "How did you find out about me, then?"

Sighing, Dina said, "There was a letter to you in their papers. I read it."

His eyebrows lifted.

She saw it and shrugged. "If you're waiting on an apology, there isn't one coming."

Reluctantly, he felt a flash of admiration for her. She was tough. He could appreciate that. She was gorgeous and he really appreciated *that*. Lust still had him by the throat and it was a wonder he could talk at all. Hard to keep his mind on what was happening when his body was urging him to think about something else entirely.

That compact yet curvy body, her dusky olive-toned skin and the wary glitter in her eyes all came together to make Connor grateful to be a man. She smelled good, too. But none of that was important right now.

"Fine," he finally managed to say. "How about a few answers, then?"

Nodding, she walked into the living room and he fol-

lowed. The house was small and old, like every other
bungalow in this section of Huntington Beach. Yards
were narrow, houses were practically on top of each other
and parking was hard to come by.

He'd noticed when he arrived that her yard was so
ratty it looked like she kept goats. The driveway had
more potholes than asphalt and the roof needed replac-
ing. The whole place could use a coat of paint and he'd
been half-afraid what the inside might look like.

But here he was surprised. The house was old but
clean. Clearly, Dina put whatever time and money she
had into maintaining the inside rather than the outside.
The hardwood floors were scarred but polished. The
walls had been painted a soft gold and boasted framed
photographs of family and nature. The furniture looked
comfortable and though the house was small, it was welcoming.

A hallway spilled from the living room and led, he
guessed, to the bedrooms. There was a small dining room
attached to the living area and beyond that, the kitchen.
A happy squeal erupted and Con flinched. The triplets
were back there. His children.

He scrubbed one hand across his face in a futile at-
tempt to clear his mind. Shaking his head, he ground out,
"My lawyer did some checking after I got your lawsuit
papers this morning."

She frowned a little, but he didn't care if she was having second thoughts about suing him now.

"He says Jackie and Elena died three months ago?"

All of the air seemed to leave her. Dina slumped and
dropped into the closest chair. "Elena was taking flying
lessons." A smile curved her mouth briefly. "She wanted

to be able to come down here to visit me and our grandmother whenever she wanted to."

Con's stomach clutched.

"Anyway, she got her license and to celebrate, she and Jackie went on a weekend trip to San Francisco."

"Without the kids?"

She nodded. "Thank God, as it turned out. One of their friends stayed at the house with the triplets. Anyway, on their way home, there was some kind of engine trouble. Elena wasn't experienced enough to compensate for it and they went down in a field."

Pain slapped at him as Connor's mind filled with memories of Jackie. Of the years they'd spent together, of the laughs, of all the good times. He hated knowing she was dead. Hated thinking how scared she must have been at the end. Hated that she wasn't here for him to yell at. Getting past his own racing thoughts, he looked at Dina and saw the misery in her eyes before she could mask it. And he was forced to remember that she'd lost her sister in that crash.

"I'm sorry," he said. "About Elena."

"Thank you," she said, taking a breath as she stood up to face him. "And I'm sorry about suing you without talking to you first."

A snort of laughter shot from his throat. "Aren't we polite all of a sudden."

"Probably won't last," she mused.

Con thought of all that had to be settled between them—of the triplets and their welfare, of his still simmering rage at having been lied to for two years—and he had to agree. "Probably not."

Nodding, Dina accepted that and asked, "So where does that put us right now?"

"Opposite sides of a fence," Connor answered.

"That's honest, anyway."

"I prefer honest. Lies always end up getting…messy." He didn't say it, but judging by Dina's expression, she heard the implication. That it was her sister and Jackie's lies that had brought them here, tangling the two of them up in a situation that was only going to get more chaotic.

Connor was here to claim his children. To do the right thing no matter who got in his way. That included Dina Cortez.

His stomach clenched as he heard a squeal of laughter soaring from the other room.

God, he was a father, and the ramifications of *that* hadn't sunk in yet. He'd only had a few hours to try to wrap his head around the fact that everything he knew had changed with the simple act of opening that envelope from Dina's lawyer.

He'd helped Jackie and Elena because he wanted to. And, he remembered, because he thought it might be fun to be on the periphery of a child's life—more as a benevolent uncle than a father. But things were different now and they'd all have to adjust.

"So, is this a truce?"

Con looked at Dina when she spoke and thought about it for a second or two. He was still angry—he didn't think that would be going away any time soon—but he had to at least bury that anger long enough to do the right thing. And that meant making sure his children were cared for. How Dina would fit into the future, he didn't know. But better to keep her close until he figured it all out.

When she shifted under his steady regard, he finally said, "Truce. For now."

A long, high-pitched wail erupted from the other room and in the next couple of seconds, two more voices joined the first until those cries built into a combined sound that ratcheted through Con's head like a hammered spike. "What the—"

Dina was already walking and threw back over her shoulder, "You want to be a father? Now's your chance."

Con swallowed back a quick jolt of nervousness and followed her. Hell, the King family had experienced a population explosion in the last few years. Every time the cousins got together, they passed kids from arm to arm, so he wasn't a stranger to crying babies. The fact that these were *his* children made the situation a little different, naturally. But he could handle it.

His babies. His children. Something visceral swamped him and he could finally understand and sympathize with everything his twin had gone through when he'd discovered his own kids. At the time, Connor had listened, sympathized and commiserated, but now he realized just what a life-altering moment this really was. Looked like he owed Colt an apology.

Yet even though he was twisted up over the circumstances they'd found themselves in, he was male enough to enjoy the view Dina provided as she walked away from him. The woman had a great behind.

Shaking his head fiercely, Connor told himself to get a grip and followed her. It wasn't far and yet it felt to him as if he was taking the longest journey of his life. From bachelor to father. From a single man to a family man.

And he wasn't sure yet just how he felt about it.

In the kitchen, he glanced around quickly, noting white walls, black counters and splashes of red in the curtains hanging over the window and the toaster and blender sitting on the counter. But it wasn't the house he was interested in right now. Instead, everything in him concentrated on the far end of the big, square room. There, behind a series of interlocked child gates, were the triplets.

One of them, a girl, stood up, wobbling a little, clutching the top rail of the gate and howling like a banshee. When she saw Dina, the tiny girl started stamping her feet as if she were marching in place. Dina swept the baby into her arms, then turned to face Connor.

"Sadie, meet your daddy."

Tears tracked along her cheeks. Wispy black curls framed her face and Connor's heart expanded so quickly, so completely, he felt a physical ache. A connection he hadn't really expected leaped to life as he looked at the tiny human being he had helped to create. Her coloring was all King, but the shape of her eyes was just like Elena's. Like Dina's. The baby stopped crying as she looked at Connor, and in a blink, she went from tears to a tiny coy smile that tugged at his heart as surely as her little fingers plucked at Dina's shirt.

Without another word, Dina handed him the baby girl, then turned to gather up the boys. She straightened with a baby on each hip, clinging to her shoulders. "They need to be changed, and since they've already had dinner, it's bath time, followed by story time and bedtime and then the countless middle-of-the-night cry times." She tipped her head and looked at him. "You up for this?"

Sadie slapped both hands against his cheeks, then dropped her head onto his shoulder with a soft sigh. Con was toast and he knew it.

"I'm up for it."

* * *

Dina had to give it to him.

She hadn't expected Connor to know a thing about handling babies. First, because he was a man, and sexist it might be, but in her experience the only thing a man knew about kids was how to hand them off to the nearest woman. Secondly, didn't the rich hire nannies so they didn't *have* to know how to care for a baby?

But he'd surprised her. Again. The first big surprise of the day had come when he'd shown up at her house unannounced and snarly yet still managing to look edible. Through their uncomfortable first meeting, the anger on both sides and the still simmering distrust, Dina had felt the unmistakable sizzle of desire.

Oh, it wasn't a good idea, but what woman wouldn't feel it? Tall, with broad shoulders, narrow hips and long legs, Connor King was the kind of man who captured attention as easily as he breathed. His black hair was a little too long, hanging over the collar of his white shirt while thick hanks of it fell across his forehead. His eyes were an icy blue and his mouth seemed to be frozen in a grim slash that only occasionally twisted into a half smile that should have been reassuring, yet wasn't. He had a right to be angry, she knew.

But he didn't have the right to be mad at *her*. She hadn't known about him until a couple of weeks ago. Okay, maybe she should have contacted him directly rather than going through lawyers, but she hadn't expected him to care. He had been a sperm donor—an untraditional one, yes, but nothing more.

Though her sister had never told Dina who the babies' father was, she had said that he'd made the donation and then disappeared from their lives. That was their story.

Of course Elena hadn't bothered to tell Dina that Connor didn't *know* about the children he'd fathered. She winced and silently acknowledged just how complicated this whole thing really was.

Until she'd read the letter that Jackie left for Connor, Dina had assumed he wasn't interested in a relationship with his kids. Which was why she had been so furious when she discovered who the babies' father really was. Because of the secret kept by Jackie and Elena, Dina had been scrambling to take care of the children when it hadn't been necessary.

Connor King was so wealthy that providing for the triplets would be easy compared to how Dina's life was going at the moment. With all the added expense of caring for the three children she was responsible for, she'd had to push her catering business to the max. She was bidding on everything from a ten-year-old's birthday party to the local bank's grand opening. Some jobs she got, some she lost.

And while getting jobs meant staying alive, she was left with the question of who took care of the kids while she worked. Dina's grandmother was always glad to help out, but the triplets were too much for the older woman to take care of on a regular basis, and paying Jamie to babysit pretty much ate up any profit Dina was lucky enough to make.

It had been a hard three months, adjusting to life as a single mom, so was it any wonder she'd sued for child support the moment she found out who the babies' father was?

A splash of water and a screech of outrage caught her attention. Gladly letting her thoughts slide away to be examined later, Dina stepped over the threshold into the cottage's one bathroom. The triplets were in the tub, Connor hanging over it, his sleeves rolled up to his elbows as he tried to deal with all three wet, slippery babies. Puddles gathered on the floor and under the knees of his slacks.

"Don't take the ducky from your sister," he said and relieved one baby of the duck in question.

A howl of outrage followed and Connor said quickly, "Here, um, which one are you? Sam? Sage? Have a boat."

Dina laughed softly, enjoying seeing someone else fight the battle of the bath for a change. Sadie loved the water, Sage spent bath time trying to escape it and Sam would fall asleep sitting up in the warm water if you weren't careful. Sadie splashed again and laughed in delight when Connor yelped as the water hit his eyes.

"Okay, little girl, no fair splashing when I'm trying to get hold of your brother."

Sadie babbled at him while Sage climbed up Connor's chest, a wet, wriggling mass eager to be out of the tub. Connor grabbed one towel, wrapped it around the tiny boy, and said, "Stay right there."

Then he turned his back on Sage to reach for the next baby. Sadie scooted out of reach, so it was Sam who was the next one out and wrapped like a burrito in a soft, dark blue towel.

Dina just watched. Sure, she could grab the boys and lend Connor a hand, but this was more interesting. She wanted to see how he reacted to the nightly ritual. If he'd fold or rise to the occasion.

While Connor reached out to grab Sadie, Sage dropped his towel and ran past Dina into the hallway, giggling all the way.

"Wait! Come back here!" Connor lifted Sadie,

wrapped her up and swung around. His gaze met Dina's and he said, "Well, thanks for the help." Frowning, he looked past her into the hallway, swinging his hair out of his eyes. "Where'd he go?"

She shrugged and smiled wider. Couldn't help herself. "Where he always goes. To the toy box in their room."

"Great," Connor said, holding onto Sadie while she squirmed, trying to get back into the water. Sweeping Sam up into his arms as well, Connor stood and faced her.

He was dripping wet. His white shirt was soaked through and plastered to what looked like a very impressive chest. Water droplets rolled down his face and clung to his hair. She smiled again. How could she not?

"Did you enjoy the show?"

"Oh, a lot," she assured him, still grinning. "But the show's not over yet. There are still three naked babies to diaper, put into jammies and settle down for bed."

He shifted the two on his hips. "And you think I can't do it?"

"I know you can't," she said, leaning against the door-jamb, folding her arms across her chest. "Not on your own."

Sadie squirmed; Sam grabbed a handful of Connor's hair and tugged. "Wanna bet?"

From the other room came Sage's high-pitched squeals and the sound of a little truck being pushed across the floor. Dina bent down, picked up the discarded towel and tossed it over Connor's shoulder. He'd had a rough go of it, but he was still standing, and she had to admire him for that. Still, she had the feeling he was about done.

"Absolutely," she said, enjoying the harried expression on Connor's face. She'd known him less than four hours, but she knew that harried wasn't a look he often wore. This was a man who ruled his world. He was used to people jumping to do his bidding. Now he had to deal with three babies who were used to calling the shots. He was in so much trouble. "What's the bet?"

A slow, seductive smile curved his mouth and Dina's insides shivered in response. Maybe betting with Connor King wasn't the smartest move she could make.

He hefted both babies a little higher and then said, "When I win, we sit down with a glass of wine and talk about where we go from here."

"And when I win, you write a check and disappear?"

The smile on his face faded away and Dina thought she'd gone too far. But what did he expect? She'd known him just a few hours and he'd crashed into her home, her family and taken over as if he had the right—which he didn't. Not from where she was standing.

He took a step closer and she kept her gaze on his. Still holding the babies close, he said, "It won't be that easy, Dina. I'm not going anywhere, so you'd better get used to it."

"And if I can't?" she asked.

"I'm willing to bet you can."

Three

Dina really didn't want to be impressed, but she was.

When the triplets first came to live with her, she'd been completely lost and practically hopeless at caring for them. She hadn't done much babysitting as a kid and none of her friends had children, so she'd had zero experience. But she'd consoled herself with the fact that most first-time moms were as lost as she herself was. Since she didn't have any choice but to jump in and do the best she could, Dina had learned as she went. She hadn't so much gotten the babies into a routine as she'd gotten herself into one. She'd had to learn from scratch—and fast—how to take care of three babies, and she'd made too many mistakes to count.

Then Connor King arrived, jumped into the fray like a natural and handled it all. He'd seemed so darn sure of himself, she'd stood back, prepared to gleefully watch a disaster unfold. Instead, he'd taken charge, as he probably did in every other aspect of his life, and gotten the job done. Sure, he was a little harried, but he'd done it. Babies were bathed and dressed and tucked into their beds with a story read by Connor, complete with sound effects that had them all giggling.

And honestly, that's what irritated her the most. The babies *liked* him. She was here day in and day out and one visit from a handsome stranger and all three of them were won over. What happened to loyalty to good old Aunt Dina, she wanted to know.

As she watched from the nursery door, she felt a small niggle of worry as Connor moved from crib to crib, smoothing his hand across the babies' heads, each in turn. He was taking a moment—what he probably thought was a private moment—to really look at the children he'd helped to create. She thought she understood what he might be feeling right then, as she'd had a very similar moment herself when the trips had come to live with her. To her, it had felt like a wild mixture of protectiveness and the realization that her life as she had known it was over.

She hadn't planned on having custody, obviously, but now Dina loved those babies with a fierceness she wouldn't have believed possible. They were her family. Her only real family now, except for her grandmother and a handful of distant cousins. She would do whatever was necessary to take care of the trips and to protect them from being hurt. Even if that meant protecting them from the man who had only wanted to be a part-time father.

By the time the evening was over, Connor was wet, exhausted and wanted nothing more than a cold beer, his bed and complete silence for ten or twelve hours. One out of three, he told himself wryly, wasn't too bad.

He took a long drink of the beer Dina'd given him and let the cold froth slide through him, easing away the tension that had had him in its grip for the last couple of hours.

"So," Dina said and he heard the grudging respect beneath her words, "you won the bet."

He managed to turn his head to look at her. "I always do, honey."

Her eyebrows lifted. "Honey?"

His lips quirked. The offhanded *honey* had slipped out, but now that he saw how annoyed she was by it, he pushed it a little further, just for the hell of it. "Babe?"

She inhaled sharply and hissed out a breath. "Dina will do."

"Right." He tipped his head and hid his smile. Connor had only known her for a few hours, but he'd already seen how easy it was to rub her the wrong way. And, for reasons he couldn't quite identify yet, he really enjoyed pushing her buttons. There was just something about this woman that urged him to push against her boundaries. "I'll remember that, Dina. Just as you should remember that when I say I'm going to do something, I do it."

"Noted."

"Good. I'm too tired to say it again." He leaned his head against the back of the couch and thought about plopping his feet on the footstool, but he was too beat to lift his own legs. "Those three are something else. Just keeping them all in the tub wore me out. I don't know how you do the whole bath and changing thing every night all alone."

"I bathe them one at a time."

He looked at her again and noticed a smile tugging at her mouth. Apparently he wasn't the only one enjoying himself. "And you didn't think that worth mentioning?"

"Well, you seemed so confident of your abilities…" She sipped at a glass of wine. "I didn't want to interfere."

"Uh-huh." He shook his head. "Well played."

"Thanks, but you got through it anyway. It was hard, but you did it. I hate to admit it, but I'm sort of impressed." She studied her wine, sliding her fingertips up and down the long, delicate crystal stem until Connor had to look away from her before he embarrassed himself. "You don't strike me as the type to know much about kids."

"I didn't," he acknowledged. "Until two years ago. My brother Colt discovered he was the father of twins. So watching him, I picked up a lot. But *three* seems like a lot more than two. Still, I gave him a lot of grief—made jokes about just how demented his life had become," he mused. "Now I feel bad about that."

"Two years?"

She'd caught that. He looked at her again and sighed. "Yeah. Right after Colt reconnected with his kids, Jackie came to me asking for help." He paused for another drink of his beer. Maybe he'd been delusional, but at the time, he'd thought it could be fun. Help Jackie and give himself a sort-of family like Colt had, only without all the hassles and the interruptions to the way he wanted to live. "Getting to know my niece and nephew is probably what pushed me into agreeing to this whole deal."

"No, that wasn't it."

One eyebrow winged up. "Is that right? Know me so well, do you? After three whole hours?"

"No," she said. "I don't know you. But Jackie did.

And she told me all about how tight you guys were. I heard all sorts of stories about you before the wedding."

That was disconcerting. He knew next to nothing about Dina. Hell, he barely remembered speaking to her at the wedding. And Connor really didn't care for being at a disadvantage.

Warily, he asked, "What kind of stories?"

She laughed a little and he thought that probably wasn't a good sign.

"The one about the redhead comes to mind," she admitted.

Surprised, he choked out a laugh. "She was a beauty," he admitted. "But we made a pact that neither of us would hit on her since we both wanted her."

"You cared more for your friendship."

He frowned. "Yeah. Back then, anyway. Apparently, things changed when I wasn't looking."

"Jackie loved you."

Con snapped her a quick, hard look. He didn't need her to tell him about Jackie. Or maybe he did. Everything he'd known was tossed into a high wind at the moment and he wasn't sure of anything anymore. But he wasn't going to talk about Jackie now. Not while his anger was so fresh and raw.

"Yeah," he muttered instead, "I'm convinced."

"All I'm saying is that you and Jackie were really tight. That's why you helped. For her. It had nothing to do with your niece and nephew. You did it for Jackie."

"Reid and Riley played a part, but yeah," he said, voice cold, "she was my best friend. Or so I thought."

In the flood of information that had hit him today, he'd hardly had time to react to any of it. The triplets had taken first priority in his mind, because they were here and the immediate problem of dealing with them was hanging over his head. But the truth was, Jackie's loss was at the back of his mind at all times.

He hated knowing she was gone. That he'd never see her again. And mostly, he hated the fact that he hadn't kept in touch with her when she and Elena moved. Not just because then he would have known about the babies, but because Jackie had been a huge part of his life from the time they were teenagers and now he just missed her, damn it. She had cut him out, true, but he hadn't called. Hadn't asked what was going on. Why she wasn't calling. Instead, he'd let it go by telling himself that it was *her* doing, and that wasn't true at all.

Over the years, whenever he had gone silent, Jackie had been the one to call and demand to know what was happening in his life. To say, *Hello? You alive?* But when she pulled back, he'd never said a word. He hadn't called. He'd assumed that she was through with him and he let it go.

Granted, friendships didn't always last. Even the best of friends eventually hit a bump too big to navigate around and ended up drifting apart. But he hadn't expected it to happen to him and Jackie. Now she was gone and he would never be able to talk to her again. To tell her he was sorry that he hadn't called to find out what she was going through.

"I don't agree with what they did either," Dina said softly, as if she knew what he was thinking.

He shot her a look, bothered by the fact that she seemed to read him so easily. "They didn't lie to you, though. They didn't deliberately cut you out of their lives."

"No," she said. "They didn't. But Elena kept things from me, too. She never told me your name."

He sat up straighter, rested his forearms on his thighs and cradled his beer bottle between his palms. He'd been a secret all the way around. In spite of what Jackie had said to him in the beginning, they might as well have gone to a sperm bank, because he had become an anonymous donor anyway. He was DNA handily acquired and soon forgotten.

There was a slap in the face as well as the heart. Damn it, why had Jackie done it? And why did he care? Whatever her reasons, they couldn't make up for what his reality was now. Anger churned into a nasty brew inside him until it was hard to draw a breath and impossible to take another swallow of beer without choking on it.

Connor needed some time to think. To plan. To gather the wildly racing thoughts circling his mind. Being here, with the kids, with the woman who was too much a distraction, wasn't helping him lay out the immediate future.

Connor liked knowing how things were going to play out. In the business he shared with Colt, Con was the guy who always thought two steps ahead. He laid out the path for their company to follow. He was the one who always knew what was coming next.

Until now.

Now he could only go with his gut. "I'll be needing a paternity test."

She sucked in a gulp of air. "You really think that's necessary?"

"No," he said shortly. Hell, all it had taken was one look at the triplets to convince him they were his. They weren't identical, of course, but each of them had the distinctive King coloring. It was more than that, though.

He'd felt a connection to those children right from the first and that was something he couldn't deny.

"My lawyers will want it," he said, not liking having to explain himself.

"Fine. Then what?"

"Then," he said, setting the beer onto the closest table before standing up, "we'll do what comes next."

"And what's that?" She stood, too, but kept her distance.

"I'll let you know."

"I think you mean we'll decide what that is together."

He laughed shortly. "I meant what I said. Those triplets in there are mine. They're Kings. I'll do the deciding here."

Her cheeks flushed with color and he knew it wasn't a blush but fury that fed the rosiness blooming across her face. "I'm their legal guardian," she reminded him. "My *sister* and her wife wanted the babies in my care."

Con didn't have the time or the patience to fight this battle right now. "And your sister and her wife *hid* my children's existence from me. For all I know, you were in on it."

"I told you I wasn't."

"And I should believe you."

She gulped in air. "Yeah, you should. Why would I lie?"

"Why would Jackie?" he countered and when she didn't have an answer for that, he nodded sharply. "Right. Anyway. I'll want time with the triplets while things are being settled."

She nodded. "I thought you would."

"And I want the letter Jackie left for me."

Her features went stiff and cool, as if she were deliberately shutting off her emotions. He couldn't blame her, because he wished to hell he could do the same. But everything he was feeling was too close to the surface. Too damn inflamed and sensitive to be buried—so instead he had to fight to push them aside.

Without another word, Dina walked across the room to a small secretary table holding a cobalt-blue bowl of fresh flowers. Connor joined her and waited as she opened the top drawer, withdrew an envelope, then handed it to him. Once she had, she crossed her arms over her chest again in what was obviously a self-protective stance.

Too bad she didn't know that whenever she did it, all she really managed to do was hike her breasts up even higher, demanding his attention. Slowly, he lifted his gaze to meet hers.

"Look," she said, "we didn't get off to the best start, but I think we can both agree that we want what's best for the triplets."

Con looked from her to the envelope for a long minute, then tucked it carefully into his inside jacket pocket. He wasn't going to read it here, with an audience.

"We do agree on that much," he allowed, then added, "but we might have different ideas as to what the *best* actually is."

"I guess we'll have to work on that when the time comes, then."

"Yeah." He had no intention of working things out. Those were *his* children, not hers. *He* would decide what was going to happen from here on out and she could either go along with it or not. Her choice. Still, for now, he would keep communications open between them. No point in making an enemy this early in the game.

"I'm gonna go," he said. "I'll be in touch."

"What's that mean?"

Her question stopped him halfway across the room. He turned back to her. "It means, we're not done. Not by a long shot."

Over the next few days, Dina tried to keep the trips on the already shaky schedule she'd had going for the last three months. But it wasn't easy, considering that Connor dropped in and out of their lives with no warning. He showed up for breakfast one morning, then went with them to a local lab where the tech took cheek swabs of each child to compare their DNA with Connor's. It was ridiculous.

He knew darn well those babies were his, so she wasn't sure what he was up to with the paternity test. The next day, he didn't show up until bath time and left as soon as the babies were put to bed. Today, he'd insisted on going to the park with them. Rather than let him have the triplets all to himself—because, really, he was *very* rich, and how did she know he wouldn't just take them to his house and refuse to give them back— she went with them.

Watching Connor interact with the triplets was endearing and irritating all at once. She had had to do a lot of adjusting when the babies had come into her life. But Connor seemed to be sailing through it. But it wasn't only that she was bothered by. He was ignoring her completely.

Not that she wanted his attention, because at this point it would only add to the confusion of the situation. But it was the principle of the thing, really. She might as well have been the babies' sixty-year-old nanny for all the awareness he showed her. Just as well, she reminded herself sternly. Dina had deliberately kept her distance from men like Connor King for most of her life. She'd seen, up close and personal, just what a strong man could do to a woman.

Her own mother had wasted her life trying to change to be whatever the man she was with at the moment wanted or needed. Helen Cortez had slowly faded away, losing herself in the never-ending quest to please a man. Dina had watched as her mother eventually lost her own identity as she depended on man after man to take care of her. Which they never did. By the time Helen died eight years ago, she was just a shadow of herself.

In response to how her mother had lived and died, Dina had vowed to be independent. To count on no one but herself. Strong men could swallow a woman whole, and she had no intention of being devoured. So it wasn't as though she *wanted* Connor—her pride was wounded, that was all.

Frowning slightly, she shifted her gaze from Connor and the triplets to the tablet on her lap. While he played with the kids, Dina took the opportunity to go over business files. An independent business owner had to stay on top of things, especially when the bottom line was looking less than enthusiastic.

Flipping through her calendar, she made notes on the different jobs listed there. She still had to contact the Johnsons about the menu for their anniversary party and then put in a bid on a big class reunion being held at the Hyatt at the end of the month. She had a wedding reception to cater in two weeks and a sixteenth birthday party three days later. None of the jobs she had lined up were exactly high paying, but she was in no position to turn a job down, either. She just wished she had more time to devote to growing her business. Instead, she spent most of her waking hours trying to get more jobs and handling the millions of details that seemed to crop up with depressing regularity.

She had thought running her own business would give her freedom. Instead, she was being strangled by all the tiny strings that were forever coming undone. She spent more time on bookkeeping and client hunting than she did actually cooking anymore, and she really missed that. But between taking care of the babies, worrying about Connor's new role in their lives and paying the bills that never stopped coming, who had time to cook?

A shriek of pain grabbed her. Dina looked up and saw Connor holding Sage while the baby screamed and cried wildly. Tossing her tablet to the park bench, she raced across the sand, feet sliding on the uneven ground until she reached Connor. When Sage lunged at her, she grabbed him, held him close and instantly began to soothe his tears. The tiny boy's breath shuddered in and out of his lungs as tears streaked his cheeks. Patting his back and rocking side to side, she looked up at Connor. "What happened?"

"He fell. He scooted out of the swing and fell about a foot to the sand." Con lifted Sadie out of the baby swing and set her in the sand beside Sam.

Sage's howls had died down to whimpers now and he snuggled his face into the curve of her neck.

"He was okay, I swear. I don't know how he moved that fast in the first place, but he was okay. In fact, he laughed at first. Then, you'd have thought he'd landed on broken glass," Connor was saying.

Dina shook her head. Finally, a chink in the perfect father armor. "He's not hurt. He's scared." She slid the palm of her hand up and down Sage's back. "He's not used to the swings and he's too small to be in a regular one anyway…"

Connor frowned, muttered, "I should have known that." Then he bent to look at Sage. "Hey, buddy, you okay?"

Sage only burrowed closer to Dina and she gave him an extra squeeze for it. The triplets might be enamored by the new man in their lives, but clearly when they wanted comforting, it was *her* they turned to. Her heart swelled with love for the three tiny people who had brought such contained chaos into her life.

"Is he all right?" Connor asked with a sigh.

"He's fine," she said. "But it's nap time, so I should get them home."

"Right." Connor nodded, his expression thoughtful. "Home."

Still holding Sage tight, Dina turned to pick up their things and head to the car. But first she glanced over her shoulder and said, "You might want to stop Sam from eating sand."

"What?"

She smiled, listening to Connor's frantic yelp as he dealt with his sand-eating son.

Con still hadn't read Jackie's letter.

He'd planned to, that first night, but he'd been too angry at her to read whatever it was she had to say. Too twisted up over his first visit with his kids and too distracted by thoughts of Dina. Besides, how could Jackie possibly explain away lying to him about his own children? There was no reason good enough, he told himself.

No excuse that would take away the pain and the fury of the betrayal still raging inside him.

For years, Jackie was the one woman he'd trusted. The one friend he could count on no matter what. To find out now that she'd used him just as so many other women had tried to tore at him.

Con wandered through his darkened house. He didn't need lights since he knew the position of every stick of furniture in the place. He didn't *want* lights because right now his mood was so dark that light would be offensive. The quiet was overpowering—especially after having been in Dina's tiny, too crowded bungalow only an hour ago. A smile teased his mouth briefly as he remembered the chorus of noises created by the busy triplets and for a second, he tried to imagine those sounds here, in his big, empty house.

"Funny," he murmured, just to shatter the silence, "this place never seemed empty before. Just…roomy."

Sure, he knew a man alone didn't need a huge house. But why buy a small one? Con had always had some vague, nebulous idea of finding a woman at some point, getting married and having kids. But he'd been in no rush for that. Now he had the kids, but no wife—just two women on his mind. The memory of one haunting him and the other, one he couldn't stop wanting.

He walked through the living room, skirted the wide coffee table and stepped through a set of French doors onto the patio. Out here, there were solar lights circling the area, but the illumination was so pale, he didn't really mind it. Barefoot, he felt the cold damp of the flagstones beneath his feet and accepted the chill as part of the June night. Moonlight sifted through a covering bank of clouds and lay across the dark ocean like a pale ribbon tossed on top of black velvet. The pounding waves slamming into the cliffs below were a heartbeat. The wind off the sea was cold and cut right through the fabric of his T-shirt, but he didn't care. He had too much to work out to bother about being cold.

For three days, he'd been the part-time father he'd thought he would be. Coming and going from the lives of the triplets and Dina like a ghost. He could drop in, harass Dina a little, play with the kids, then leave it all behind and go to his office. There, his new responsibilities were buried beneath contracts, dealing with clients, new business ventures and a hundred other things that demanded his attention.

But always, the triplets and their guardian came sliding back into his consciousness. And every time he left that cottage in Huntington Beach, it was harder to go. Con scraped one hand across the back of his neck as that realization sank in. However it had started—outrage, betrayal, duty—it had become something else. What, exactly, he wasn't ready to admit yet. But he knew he was deeper into this situation than he would have thought possible three days ago. He knew that he missed those kids when he wasn't around them.

And yeah, he missed being around Dina, too. Damn, but the woman was fascinating. She was on edge around him most of the time, but that didn't do anything to dull the desire he felt every time he looked at her. She was prickly, defensive and her temper made those dark brown eyes of hers flash. Damned if he didn't enjoy that, too.

Then there was today at the park. When Sage was hurt and scared, he hadn't wanted Con. He'd wanted Dina. Her connection to the babies was deep despite the fact that she'd been their guardian only three months. So

Con had to work with that, as well. Did he take those kids away from her? Or did he try to find a way to work with her?

"Hell, this whole mess could have been avoided if Jackie had just told me the damn truth." He tipped his head back, stared up at the sky and said, "You know you did this, right? You enjoying the show?"

He couldn't get an answer from the night. The only one he might get was in the house, in Jackie's letter. And it was time to finally read it. See what his friend had to say to him.

Whatever it is, it's too little, too late, as his mother used to say.

Shaking his head, Con stalked across the patio to the house, then walked into his bedroom and snatched Jackie's letter off the dresser. He hit the wall switch, flooding the huge room with light from the ironwork chandelier overhead. He took a seat on the edge of his bed and pulled the letter free. His gaze swept over the familiar handwriting and in his head, he heard Jackie's voice…

"Con, if you're reading this, Elena and I are both gone, so no offense, but I hope you never read this. But if you are, I know you're pissed, and I can't blame you. Yes. I lied."

Anger spat at him again.

"I didn't tell you about the pregnancy or the babies because Elena and I wanted them all to ourselves. Yeah, selfish. I can almost hear you thinking it. And maybe it was, I don't even know. But when you said you wanted to be a part of the babies'

*lives, it made both of us realize that you would
only confuse things.*

*"Wasn't it enough that they would have two
mommies? Did they really need an on-again, off-
again daddy, too? Besides, we both know babies
aren't really your thing. Remember how you gave
Colt such a hard time over the twins? We named
Dina guardian because of the usual sexist reasons."*

Connor laughed in spite of himself.

*"She's a girl. Kids need a mommy. Sue me. Give
her a chance. You might like her.*

*"Con, I didn't want you to think you had to sup-
port them. Or had to do a damn thing. You'd already done enough. You gave us our family and
we're grateful. We gave you your freedom because
we thought it was best.*

*"But never doubt that we thought of you every
day. Every time we looked into the triplets' faces,
there you were. So forgive me if you can—and if
you can't, I understand. I still love you—Jackie."*

Pain swamped the anger and for the first time in days,
Con felt calm. She was wrong to do it, but he understood.
He didn't want to forgive her, but how could he not?

Holding the letter, he smoothed his fingertip across
the boldly slanted writing and murmured, "I love you,
too, Jacks."

Four

"Jackie made it clear in her letter that they wanted Dina to have custody," Colt said quietly when he'd finished reading it. He handed the paper over to Con, who stared at it for a long minute.

"They're *my* kids, Colt. My blood."

Con couldn't get past that one truth, which kept repeating over and over in his mind, and honestly, he didn't want to. After reading Jackie's letter the night before, his thoughts hadn't been able to settle. He hadn't slept and he was just killing time here at work. God knew there were details of new contracts to work out, but how the hell could he concentrate on that when the bulk of his life was up in the air?

He hadn't forgiven Jackie for what she'd done. Did he understand why she did it? A part of him did. The cool, rational, logical voice in his mind could even agree with her. But the reality was, emotion was running the show right now. And he couldn't get past the fact that he'd lost more than a year of his children's lives. He'd never get it back. He was a visitor in that house near the beach. A stranger. And that just burned him.

Behind him, there was a wide window, offering a spectacular view of the beach and the ocean, but it might as well have been a blank wall for all the attention he'd paid it that morning. Sunlight streamed through the tinted glass, painting the office a soft gold that glittered in his twin's eyes as Colt stared at Connor, waiting.

Finally, Con spoke again. "You know that Sage hates taking a bath?"

"What?" Colt frowned at him.

"Sage. He hates the water. Why? I should know that, but I don't." He pushed out of his desk chair and stalked around the perimeter of his office. It was a plush room with thick carpeting, framed photographs of their many adventure sites dotting the walls and comfortable furniture for clients. "Sadie loves taking a bath. She splashes and squeals." He smiled to himself, remembering. "Sam couldn't care less either way, but Sage…" He shook his head, then whipped a look at Colt. "Did something happen to him? Did he get scared? Of what? By who?"

"You're overreacting, Con," his twin said. "Kids are wildly unpredictable. Who the hell knows what they're thinking or why they react to things the way they do? Trust me on this. Like, for instance, right now, Reid won't wear shoes." He laughed to himself. "Takes 'em off the minute you put them on him. It's driving Penny nuts. But maybe it's because last week he walked through a deep puddle and his sneakers were squishing. I think he hated the sound so much, it creeped him out."

"See?" Con jabbed a finger toward his twin as fresh fury erupted inside him. "That's what I'm saying. Reid has an issue and you know why! Sage hates water, I don't have a clue." He threw his hands up in frustration. "I've known my own kids for three lousy days. I'm a damn stranger to them, Colt. They're nuts about Dina and they don't even know me."

"That'll change," Colt told him.

"Damn straight it will." Con jammed his hands into his pockets and rocked back on his heels. The wheels were in motion now and things should start happening.

After reading Jackie's letter, he'd been up all night. And this morning, he'd made his decision. He'd called his lawyers, telling them to put together whatever it was they had to do to get him custody of the triplets. But his lawyer had told him that Dina had good ground to stand on, too. She was the legal guardian. The kids' aunt. They were settled with her. But it didn't have to stay that way.

"You've already called Murdoch and Sons in on this, haven't you?"

Con shot his brother a sly smile. "Best team of lawyers in the state."

"Yeah, I know," Colt said, standing up to face his brother. "But think about it for a minute. Remember how mad you were when Dina went through a lawyer and sued you instead of just talking to you?"

"Yeah, I remember." His scowl deepened. "This is different."

"Always is," Colt muttered, then said more loudly, "You can't cut Dina Cortez out of this, Con."

He shot his twin a hard look. "What makes you think I'm considering it?"

Colt laughed shortly. "Because I know you? Because

when I found out about Penny and the twins, that was *my* first thought?"

"Okay." Con rubbed the back of his neck. Maybe he had thought of it, but he was willing to be reasonable about all this. If she fought him on custody, though, he wouldn't make any promises. This would all be a lot easier if he didn't want Dina so much. Every time he saw her it was harder to keep his hands off her—but this was about the kids and he had to keep focused.

"You think you can pull it off." Colt shook his head. "Delusional. That usually doesn't happen until you start losing sleep because of the kids invading your life. But kudos for managing on your own."

"Funny."

"Seriously, Con, she's not just their guardian, she's their *aunt*. You really think she's going to just walk away because it would be easier on you?"

"No." He sat back and shook his head. "The last thing she wants to do is make anything easy on me."

"There you go. This means you're going to have to find a way to work with her—or around her."

Con slanted him a look. "As in..."

Colt shrugged, "As in, you could try buying her off."

Frowning, Connor thought about that for a minute or two.

He'd seen her house. It was too small and gave every indication that money was tight. According to his lawyer, her catering business was barely above water. He knew she couldn't afford to take care of the babies on her own, and he wasn't about to settle for being nothing more than a monthly check in the lives of his kids.

According to the King family lawyer, the best thing for him to do, as far as a custody hearing went, was to become an everyday part of the children's lives. To stake a claim, basically. Well, that worked for Con. He just had to figure out the best way to go about it.

The easiest way, of course, would be to bring the triplets to his place. He already had his housekeeper setting up a temporary nursery in one of the guest rooms. A more permanent room was in the works, too. Their cousins Rafe, Nick and Gavin owned King Construction and Con was going to have them build a full nursery suite for the triplets as soon as possible. Meanwhile, the rest of Con's house was being babyproofed as well. He'd seen what Colt and Penny had gone through at their house, making sure everything was safe for a set of curious twins, so he had a good idea of what was needed.

The obstacle to overcome would be Dina. But he had an idea on that, as well.

"Whose side are you on in this, anyway?"

"Yours." Colt lifted both hands in the classic surrender pose and smiled at his brother. "I'm just saying that if you try to cut Dina out, you're inviting open war, and once that happens, nobody wins."

"I'll win."

"Really?" Colt shook his head and stood up. "She's their aunt, Con. You cut her out, the kids get hurt. You become enemies and this battle will get uglier and uglier."

"That's the thing though," Con said. "It *is* a battle. Or will be as soon as Dina realizes I'm not taking a backseat in all this. Damn it, if Jackie—"

"Let it go already," Colt muttered. "Jackie did what she thought she had to and so will you."

"Damn right I will."

"But you *could* listen to your older and wiser brother."

Con snorted. "Five extra minutes of life makes you the expert?"

"No," Colt corrected. "Going through practically the same thing you are and surviving makes me the expert. Penny and I were able to work things out between us—"

"Yeah, but you were already in love with Penny, you just didn't want to admit it."

"Good point and yeah, I know you don't love Dina." Colt gave him a grin. "But you do *want* her."

Did he ever. The desire he'd felt for her from the start had become a *need* that he really didn't want to admit to, because it just made everything else that much more convoluted. But just thinking about Dina made him hard and hungry.

"Mess this up and you'll never have her."

"Fine, fine." Con waved one hand at his twin. He hated to admit that his brother had a point. "Don't make her an enemy. Go slow." He paused. "I don't like slow."

"You're not used to it, that's for sure."

"True." He pushed one hand through his hair. "I want to get moving on this but I know I've got to make the right steps."

"That's something, anyway," Colt said wryly.

"I got the DNA results," Con said.

"That was fast."

"Money talks." Ordinarily, it would have taken a week, maybe two, to get the results from the private lab. But with the King family fortune pushing buttons, it had only been days. He paused. "The kids are mine."

"You had a doubt?"

"Of course not. But now it's legal. It's ammunition for a custody fight."

"Con…"

"I know, avoid a fight if I can." He held up one hand to stop his brother before he could get going again. "And I will. But I like knowing I've got an ace in the hole."

"Okay, clearly you're going at this full tilt and nothing I say is going to make any difference," Colt said. "So I'm going to say one more thing."

"Naturally."

"Go easy on this or you'll lose."

"You're wrong. I don't lose."

"I'm really sorry, Abuela," Dina said, "but the babysitter canceled on me at the last minute and I have to be at this party." She unloaded all of the supplies she'd brought for the triplets as her grandmother sat on the floor, playing with the babies.

"Dina, you don't have to apologize," she said, throwing her granddaughter a quick glance over her shoulder. "I love having the children here."

"Yeah, but you were going to dinner with your friends."

"Pish. I can eat anytime." She reached out and caught Sage up in a quick hug. "It's not every day I get snuggles from *los niños*."

Dina smiled as the triplets crawled all over the older woman. At seventy-five, Angelica Cortez was trim, with stylishly cut gray hair that swung at her jawline. Her brown eyes were shrewd and her striking face remained remarkably unlined, which gave Dina hope for her own future.

Angelica's English was lightly flavored with her native Mexico; Spanish and English mingled happily in everything she said. She did love seeing the babies and if Dina and the kids were here strictly for a visit, it would be different. Dina would be here, too, taking care of them rather than expecting her grandmother to pick up the slack. But with her babysitter sick, Dina just didn't have a choice. She was catering an anniversary party tonight and if it went well, there was a chance she'd get more jobs out of it.

A headache began to blossom behind her eyes and that didn't bode well for the long night she had ahead of her. Guilt pinged around inside her like a crazed Ping-Pong ball. Guilt for leaving the kids, for making her grandmother change her own plans to watch them—and then there was the guilt for choosing work over the babies. But on the other hand, if she wanted to be able to feed them, she had to get as many jobs as she could.

Her grandmother's duplex in Naples was two blocks from the ocean. It was decorated in a blend of Mexican and American styles and was warm and inviting. Furniture was overstuffed; the walls were painted a rich brick red with white crown molding. It should have been dark and depressing, Dina had thought more than once. Instead, it was like being enveloped in a hug. Angelica owned the building and lived in the front apartment while renting the second to one of her best friends. Between the two women, the gardens were so lush and beautiful, they regularly had tourists stopping out front to take pictures.

Naples was small, and elegant, and there were canals winding through the neighborhood much like its Italian namesake. The Christmas parade through the canals was amazing, with the houses and boats decorated with millions of colored lights. Dina was looking forward to taking the triplets to see the spectacle.

"So what is the job tonight?"

"An anniversary party in Newport Beach."

Which was about a half hour away, and that meant Dina would have to leave soon to get to the site early enough to set up.

Not too long ago, Dina had been the owner of a great little food truck. Business had been good enough that she'd decided to move on and open the catering business she'd always wanted. And it had been doing well, too. She'd had more jobs than she could count, her reputation was growing—and then...

She looked to where the babies were clustered around their great-grandmother. Dina's world had crashed every bit as much as her sister's plane had three months ago. When she had taken custody of the trips, Dina had had to cancel a lot of jobs. She simply hadn't been able to keep up the pace when faced with caring for the three kids. Though her income had been slashed, the bills hadn't stopped coming. Her rent had gone up, her car broke down, and with the triplets, there were *more* bills. Doctors, clothes, diapers—the list was never ending, and it was scary being the sole responsible one.

Now she was having to scramble to get jobs, which meant she was bidding on parties she might have ignored a few months ago. But she needed the work to take care of the babies and make sure they were safe.

"Don't worry so much, *nieta*," her grandmother said, and Dina had to smile in spite of the anxiety that never quite left her. "Things happen whether you're ready or not. You simply have to do what you can to keep up."

"Yeah," Dina said, dropping to her knees to gather Sam up into her arms. The tiny boy sagged into her, wrapping his little arms around her neck and smacking her cheek with an openmouthed kiss that left drool behind on her skin and warmth in her heart. She kissed him back, then set him down on the floor beside his brother and sister.

"You haven't spoken of their father yet."

Dina looked at her grandmother. The unsettled feeling she'd been carrying around for days deepened. Of course, she had told her grandmother about the suit for child support and the letter she'd found in Jackie's things. But she really hadn't had a chance to talk with her about it since.

Mainly because what could she say? That Connor was getting too involved for her peace of mind? That she couldn't seem to think straight when he was near? That she was worried not only about what his presence meant to the triplets—but what it meant to *her*?

He was at the forefront of her mind, always, and she hadn't been prepared for that. It had been a long time since Dina had met a man she was attracted to. And she'd *never* met one who affected her as Connor King did. It was stupid, she knew, to even indulge in idle daydreams about a man who had the power to take her children away from her. Connor made her want all sorts of things, but at the same time, she knew she should be keeping him at a safe distance. It was as if she were waiting for *two* shoes to drop. What were his plans for the kids? What were his plans for *her*?

"I don't know, Abuela," she finally said. "He really enjoys the triplets when he's with them. Naturally, he's angry. With Jackie and Elena. And with me."

Nodding sagely, the older woman said, "I told Elena what she was doing was wrong, but like you, she was *cabeza dura*. A hardhead." She paused, made the sign of the cross and whispered a quick prayer for Elena's soul, then reached out to pat Dina's hand. "His anger will pass."

"I know." Dina sighed. No one could hold on to anger

forever. It would eventually burn itself out, leaving bitterness behind, and it would be up to Connor if he chose to hang on to it or let that go as well. Right now, she thought it was a toss-up as to which way he'd go. "But what then?"

"Well, he has a decision to make, doesn't he?" her grandmother said. "He must decide how involved he wants to be with his children." Her gaze swept over the three babies playing and babbling together. "I've read of the King family. They are not the kind of people to walk away from their children."

Dina's heart sank. Different members of the King family were always in the news or the tabloids or national magazines. And in interview after interview, one thing they all had in common was just how close they were and how important family was. "I know."

Her grandmother heard the disappointment and worry in Dina's voice and laughed. "That's a good thing, *querida*. He's their father. They'll need him."

"And what about me?" She shook her head and watched as Sadie and Sam had a tug-of-war over a stuffed bunny. The thought of losing the triplets made her chest hurt. Yes, they were a lot of work, and yes, her life had been turned upside down at their arrival, but now she couldn't imagine living without them.

"The Kings are also *really* rich," she pointed out, more to herself than to her grandmother. "If he wants to take the babies from me, I won't be able to afford to fight him. He can hire a fleet of lawyers and I'll be down at Legal Aid with my fingers crossed."

Her grandmother laughed, handed a baby doll to Sadie and smiled as she watched Sam chew on the stuffed bunny's ear. "Wealthy doesn't mean evil, Dina."

"No, but it does mean powerful," she argued as worry nibbled at her insides. "No judge is going to pick a struggling caterer over a member of the King family when it comes to custody."

"Worrying won't change that," her grandmother warned.

"No, but I'm so good at it."

The older woman laughed. "Yes, you are. But just this once, you should try not to excel at something."

Dina sighed, shook her head and dropped one arm around her grandmother's shoulders, pulling her close for a brief, hard hug. "I'll try. Really."

Giving Dina another pat, her grandmother said, "This is a good thing, for you and for the babies."

"It doesn't feel that way," she said, though her hormones might have disagreed.

"Dina, you can't care for them on your own. You're making yourself crazy by trying."

"I can do it," she said stubbornly. "I'm getting a routine and—"

"And wearing yourself to the bone trying to be all things to all people," her grandmother told her quietly, almost as though she were hoping to keep the triplets from hearing—though they wouldn't have understood her anyway. "Their father is here now. Share the work as well as the joy."

"It's not that easy, Abuela," Dina said with a sigh. "He's one of the richest men in the country and he's furious at being lied to."

"You didn't lie to him."

"I don't think he cares," she said thoughtfully. "If he decides to, he could take the babies from me and no judge would ever choose me over him."

"It doesn't have to come to that."

"Maybe not, but I think it will," Dina said, remembering the look on his face the night before. He was bonding with his children and digging himself deeper into all of their lives. Connor King wasn't going to back off. It wasn't in his nature.

She'd done some checking on him. Granted, it had been on the internet and she knew you couldn't believe everything you read there. But she had no other options.

He and his twin, Colton, had built their own business outside of the family fortune. They were rich in their own right now, after spending years providing risk to thrill seekers. A little less than two years ago, the twins had shifted their business model to family vacations and hadn't missed a step. According to financial websites, King Family Adventures was even bigger than its precursor, which made sense, since their potential client base was so much bigger.

From everything she'd read, Connor was a hard, cold-eyed negotiator and didn't tolerate mistakes. He was the kind of man who laid down the rules and expected everyone else to fall into line. Since Dina didn't take orders well, she couldn't see any way this situation was going to have a happy ending.

"I see another problem on the horizon as well," Angelica said softly.

"Great. Just what we need." She blew out a breath. "What problem?"

"You like him." Her grandmother smiled knowingly.

"Please." Dina laughed and ducked her head to keep her too-knowing grandmother from reading her eyes. She grabbed Sadie as the baby toddled past and plopped the tiny girl onto her lap. "You're wrong, Abuela. I don't like him."

"So you didn't lie to him, only to me," the older woman said, "and to yourself."

Reluctantly, Dina lifted her gaze to her grandmother's. It was pointless to keep avoiding this particular truth anyway. "Fine. I admit to being…intrigued. He's so different from every other man I know. But—"

"Different is good, *mija*," she said, scooping Sadie off Dina's lap and onto her own. "And who knows? Maybe this man's arrival in your life is a good thing."

Dina wouldn't go that far.

A little after midnight, Dina pulled into her driveway with three sleeping babies in the backseat. Glancing at the house, she muttered a soft curse because she'd forgotten to leave the porch light on.

With a sigh, she climbed out of the car and then as quietly as possible closed the door behind her. The street was silent, houses dark, with families tucked in for the night. It was so quiet, it was as if the whole world had taken a breath and held it.

And then she heard a voice.

"Where the hell have you been?"

Five

Dina jumped, slapped one hand to her chest and spun around all at the same time. Heart in her throat, she watched Connor stalk across the yard toward her.

"You scared me to death," she said, her voice a harsh whisper.

"Welcome to my world," he snapped. "I've been sitting on your front porch for the last three hours, not knowing where the hell you were."

"What? Why?" She looked past him to the porch as if she could see evidence of his vigil.

"I came to see the kids, but you weren't here." He scrubbed both hands across his face, then glared at her. "I didn't know where you'd gone. For all I knew, you were out and trapped somewhere, or maybe one of the kids was sick. I called your cell and you didn't answer. Went straight to voice mail."

One small niggle of guilt wormed its way through her, but Dina dismissed it fast. How was she supposed to know that he would show up? Just because he'd been dropping by on and off for days was no reason to assume he'd keep doing it. Besides, he was overreacting and that she could hardly believe. He sounded like a worried husband, for heaven's sake.

"I always turn my phone off when I'm working," she said, though that wasn't true. She'd kept the phone on in case her grandmother needed to reach her. She simply hadn't answered the phone when she saw it was Connor calling. "And now I'm going to put the triplets to bed. They're sound asleep in their car seats and if you wake them…"

Her threat lay open-ended between them, but it did the trick. He took a breath, made an obvious effort to calm himself and said, "Fine. I'll help. Go unlock the front door."

She did it, but only because that's what she was going to do before he'd ordered her to do it anyway. Muttering under her breath, Dina crossed the yard with hurried strides. It was cold and damp and the moon and stars were blotted out behind a layer of clouds. She opened the door, then turned and headed back to the car, where Con was already unhooking Sam from his car seat. Her heart twisted a bit as the little boy draped himself across Con's shoulder, arms and legs limp in sleep. Connor kept one hand on the boy's back and walked to the house without another word to her.

Good, Dina thought. She was in no mood for his attitude. She was tired, her feet hurt and all she wanted was to sit down, have a glass of wine and then crawl into bed for the few hours' sleep she'd get before the babies woke up.

She freed Sadie from her car seat and soothed the baby girl as she snuffled, whimpered and settled down again.

"I'll take her," Connor whispered when he came up behind her.

"You get Sage," she said, already walking.

In what used to be the bungalow's master bedroom, three cribs were crowded together in the small space. It wouldn't be long before Dina would have to find somewhere else to live. The babies were going to outgrow this house within the next year or so. But that was a worry for another day.

"Why the hell didn't you answer the phone?" Connor's strained whisper sounded overly loud in the quiet.

"I was working," she reminded him. "Then when I wasn't, I turned the phone off to keep from waking up the babies on the way home."

"Okay, then," he ground out, "what kind of job are you working that you've got three babies out until after midnight?"

She frowned at him as she leaned over the crib and patted Sam's back until he settled into deep sleep again. "I was catering an anniversary party, and the babies are fine."

"They should have been home," he said, that strained whisper somehow even more strained now.

Dina swallowed her impatience. "Not that it's any of your business, but my babysitter got sick at the last minute, so my grandmother watched them for me."

While Connor soothed a snuffling, writhing Sadie, he glared at Dina. "Why the hell didn't you call me? I could have been here to watch them. Hell, I *was* here.

On the damn porch, imagining you and the babies dead in a ditch somewhere."

He was serious. She didn't know whether to be touched, amused or angry. Amusement won.

She snorted a laugh and was pleased to see his expression darken even further. "Who're you, my mother?"

"No," he reminded her. "I'm their father, and you should have answered my calls."

Looking into his eyes, she saw beyond his anger to the worry that had been dogging him for hours. If the situation had been turned around and *he* had been off with the triplets and she hadn't been able to reach him, she would have been furious, too. And worried. And scared. And her imagination would have tortured her with images of car accidents, kidnappings—heck, even space invaders!

Maybe she should have answered his calls, but the truth was, she only left her phone turned on while working in case there was an emergency with the babies. Otherwise, she was focused on the task at hand. And frankly, every time her phone rang and she saw Connor's number, she'd enjoyed shifting him to voice mail. He was so...dominant male that being able to thwart him even a little had made her feel better. Now, though, she was rethinking that decision.

"Okay, I'm sorry." Oh, that was bitter. "I should have let you know the kids were all right."

"It wasn't only them I was worried about," he said, voice deeper, lower, more intimate.

She looked at him and in the soft glow of the nightlight, his blue eyes seemed fathomless, fixed on her. She felt drawn to him. So much so that she deliberately looked away and took a step back.

The babies were settled and the baby monitor turned

on, so to continue the conversation, Dina led Connor out of the bedroom. She needed some breathing room. Flipping on light switches as she went, to dispel the dark and the accompanying intimacy, she walked straight to the living room with him following close behind. She entered the room, turned to face him and saw that he'd stopped in the open doorway. Taking a breath, she steadied herself. "I'm tired, Connor. Can we do the rest of this another time?"

Rather than answer, he asked a question of his own. "Why didn't you ask me to watch the kids?"

"The simplest answer? It never occurred to me."

A rush of pure frustration swamped Connor as he met her eyes and read the truth there. He read the fatigue in her eyes and noted the defensive posture she always adopted when they began to butt heads, and that was almost enough to defuse the anger churning inside him. The last few hours, he'd felt more helpless than he ever had, and he hadn't enjoyed it. He was used to being in charge, to knowing what was going on at all times. To be in the dark about his own children had been torture.

By the time she had pulled into the driveway, Connor had been tense enough to snap in two. It was only the presence of the sleeping babies that had kept his temper from boiling over. But his frustration continued to bubble and froth in the pit of his stomach.

She hadn't called him because she hadn't given him a thought. She'd needed help and she'd gone to her grandmother instead of him. Because he wasn't a part of her or the kids' lives. He was still on the periphery, and he was the only one who could change that.

"That's got to stop," he said flatly, silently congratulating himself on his rigid control.

"Look, I'm sorry you were worried," she said. "But I'm too tired to do this right now."

He nodded solemnly. "Fine. We'll talk about it in the morning."

"Okay, good." She waved a hand at the hall and the front door behind him. "Now I'm going to bed and you should go home."

"Oh," Connor said, leaning against the doorjamb with a casual ease he wasn't feeling, "I'm not going anywhere."

"What?"

Her chocolate eyes went wide and outraged and Connor smiled. He liked the way she went from cool to hot in a split second and he really wanted to see how hot she'd burn in his bed. For a second or two, *that* image scalded his brain and made speech impossible. When he came back to the moment, she was in the middle of a whispered rant, trying to keep her anger from waking the babies in the other room.

"You think you can just stay uninvited in my house? What gives you the right? Nothing, that's what." She answered her own question before he could say a word. She glanced at the baby monitor she held in her hands as the sounds of restless squirming cut into the room. In another moment or two, they might be awake and crying and this conversation—such as it was—would come to an end.

So he ended it first.

Connor didn't think about it, he simply went on instinct, following the urges that had been clawing at him since the first time he'd seen her. Pushing away from the wall, he grabbed her, pulled her close and kissed her.

The instant his mouth met hers, heat exploded between them. Sensations unlike anything he'd ever known before enveloped him and Connor could only hold onto her, tightening his arms around her until he held her captive, pinned to his body. She went from startled to swept away in a heartbeat. As if she, too, were being consumed by the flames licking at his insides, she hooked her arms around his neck and held on. Mouths taking, giving, tongues twining together in a frantic dance of need. Their breath came in short, hard gasps. The bright living room lights shining around them did nothing to dispel the closeness wrapping itself around them.

His brain racing, heart thundering in his chest and his groin so heavy and hard he ached with it, Connor relished the feel of her mouth under his. The longer he kissed her, the more he felt, those flames burning brighter, hotter, scorching his soul. She sighed and leaned into him, and that soft sound was enough to penetrate his brain, bring him back to himself and the realization that he was only a blink away from pulling Dina down to the damn floor.

No. When this happened, he told himself, they would have a bed. And privacy. And all the time they needed to explore whatever it was burning between them. When that thought registered, he broke the kiss, stepped back and with satisfaction, watched her stagger before finding her balance. Breath ragged in his lungs, his heart hammering against his ribs, Con ground out, "I'm staying here tonight."

She shook her head instantly. "We're not going to—"

"I'll sleep on the couch."

Her gaze met his and she must have seen that he wasn't going to be sent on his way. With tension blistering the air in the room, she only nodded, accepting the inevitable.

"This isn't over," he said.

"It is for tonight," she answered and walked past him, down the short hall to her room. She disappeared inside and closed the door behind her.

Alone, Connor shoved one hand through his hair and barely resisted giving it a hard tug to relieve some of the frustration still holding him in its clutches. Instead, he walked to the too-short couch and eyed it grimly.

It was going to be a miserable night.

During the long, incredibly sleepless night, Connor had had time to do some thinking. And some snooping. Sure, maybe he had crossed a line, when he'd poked around in Dina's laptop, which really should be password protected. But he'd told himself that the triplets gave him all the reason he needed to invade her privacy a little.

Just as his lawyers had informed him, her business was in trouble. She was already in a downward spiral of debt and picking up speed every day. He'd flipped through enough of her records to know that she was using her small savings account to supplement her income and that wasn't going to last for much longer.

Bottom line? Dina Cortez was in no shape to provide for three growing kids. And he could use that information.

He already had the babies changed and dressed when she walked into the nursery bright and early the next morning. One look was all it took to tell him that she'd gotten as little sleep during the night as he had.

"You're awake?"

He shrugged and finished pulling Sam's shirt into place. "Never really went to sleep." He shot her a sly glance. "Too much on my mind."

She inhaled sharply and Connor guessed that she'd

been thinking about that kiss and what should have come next. Hell, thoughts like that had been tormenting him all night. Knowing that she was just down the hall from him. Knowing that she would welcome his touch. It had taken everything he had to keep from going to her.

But the bottom line was that he wasn't here because of this attraction and desire he felt for Dina. He was here for his children, and they had to come first. If he made a play for Dina, it would complicate everything. Better to settle the situation here before moving on what he wanted from her.

He took a long breath himself before quipping, "Plus, that couch qualifies as torture equipment."

"Well it isn't built to sleep on," she admitted, "especially for someone as tall as you."

"That's for sure." He lifted Sam off the table, gave the baby boy a kiss, then set him on the floor with his brother and sister. "So. Kids are changed, dressed and ready for the day. How about we feed them and then we have that talk?"

"I need coffee."

"I'll take that as a yes," he said, scooping up two of the babies and leaving Sam for Dina to get. Then he walked past her, heading for the kitchen.

The room was bright with sunshine and ringing with the happy chatter of three babies. Despite being tired, Connor and Dina worked together to prepare milk, oatmeal and bananas. While they fed the triplets, Connor glanced at her and said, "Last night brought home to me that things have got to change."

"What *things*?"

He would have heard the wariness in her tone even if he hadn't spotted it on her features. "Everything about this whole situation. You. Me. The triplets. As it stands now, none of it is working for me."

She sighed and shook her head. "It's been, like, four days. You could be more patient."

"Not in my nature."

"I'm getting that," she murmured.

"Anyway, it's been long enough to make some decisions," he countered and scooped more oatmeal onto a spoon before offering it to Sadie, who opened her mouth eagerly, like a baby bird. "For instance. Your catering business—why catering?"

"What? Oh. Uh. I used to have a food truck and it did really well." She smiled, remembering. "So well, in fact, that I sold the truck to my cousin Raul. I went into catering thinking I could use that as a stepping-stone to my real goal—opening my own restaurant."

"A good goal, but hard to meet when your catering business is sinking."

"Excuse me?" She stopped moving with a spoonful of cereal halfway to Sage's mouth. The little boy howled and slapped both hands impatiently on his tray table. "Sorry, sorry, baby," she murmured and fed him before turning back to Connor. "How would you know anything about my business?"

He couldn't blame her for being mad, but he wouldn't apologize for doing what he had to do to look out for his kids. If that made the relationship between him and Dina tougher for a while, he could deal with that. Connor had the taste of her inside him now and he wouldn't stop pushing until he got more. Eventually he knew he'd have his kids and Dina, too.

But for now he said only, "First, my lawyers have a private investigator on retainer—"

"You had me investigated?"

He nodded, ignoring the shocked expression on her face because it was just going to get worse in another minute or so. "And for another, I looked through your bills last night."

"You did what?" Her voice dropped to a new level of cold that sliced at him like shards of ice. She shot a glance at her laptop, lying innocently on the counter, then looked back at him. "You went through my records?"

"I did, and if you're waiting for an apology, don't hold your breath." His gaze speared hers and he didn't flinch away from the pure rage spitting back at him. Those dark brown eyes of hers flashed with heat in spite of the cold in her voice. "You're taking care of my kids and I needed to be sure you can do that properly. As it turns out, you can't."

"Is that right? Well, I've been managing all right so far. The babies are *fine* and you know it. They're fed, they're happy, they're *loved*." She stiffened, squared her shoulders and lifted her chin. "The four of us are getting along great. You want to pay child support, I'm happy to take it for them. But I don't need your help to run my business or our lives."

Connor could admire her pride even as he dismissed it. Being proud was one thing. Being too stubborn to see the truth was another. "Of course you do, and you know it. That's why you contacted me in the first place. It's not just the money and you know it, Dina. You're running yourself into the ground trying to do everything by yourself. You're behind on your bills, and you haven't had a good paying job since before the triplets arrived."

She flushed and again, it wasn't embarrassment but anger that flooded her cheeks with color. "I admit, my business suffered some when the babies first came to me. I had to back out of jobs and spend most of my time with them. They were traumatized—not that you'd know anything about that since you weren't here—because they'd lost their parents and their home. It took weeks to get them settled into a routine. Make them feel safe."

She glared at him and those eyes of hers were damned captivating.

"I was the one who held things together. And they were my priority. I'm so very sorry if you think my business isn't doing too well." She took a breath. "Now that the kids are settled in, I'm bidding on jobs again and—"

"Birthday and anniversary parties," he finished for her. "Not exactly big-paying jobs."

Dropping her gaze, she scooped up more oatmeal and spooned it into Sage's waiting mouth. "No job too small," she said tightly. "Besides, one job leads to another. Catering is a lot about word of mouth and—"

"Admit it, Dina. You're in the water, holding onto a lead ball and trying to kick your way to the surface."

"Could you please stop interrupting me?"

"Admit it," he urged again. "At this rate, you will never reach your goal of opening a restaurant. Hell, you'll be lucky if you can keep the catering going through the rest of the year. And once it fails completely? Then what? What's your backup plan? Or do you even have one?"

Con watched her and saw in her eyes that she couldn't argue with him, but that she was going to give it a try anyway.

"These children will never suffer." She swore it, meeting his eyes, willing him to believe her. "It doesn't matter what I have to do, they will never go without."

"I know they won't," he said quietly and set small plastic bowls of sliced bananas onto the triplets' food trays. Connor waited until she turned to face him. When he had her complete attention, he said, "I'll give you two hundred and fifty thousand dollars to sign over custody of the kids to me. Right now. Today."

He saw confusion obliterated by fury in her dark eyes an instant before she exploded in a wild burst of rage. "You would *dare* to offer me *money*? You think you can *buy* me? That I would *sell my family*?"

She stood up slowly, as if every bone ached. The babies watched her with curiosity. They didn't cry, because even in her anger, Dina kept her voice a hushed whisper that somehow made her temper sound even more volatile than if she'd been shouting.

"Do it and open that restaurant you want so badly. Build your dreams. I'm offering you a way out of the financial hole you're sliding into."

"Build my dreams by selling the babies? Do you really think so little of me?"

"Not at all," he countered smoothly, refusing to match her temper. "I think you're smart, clever and wise enough to recognize a real opportunity when it presents itself."

She choked out a laugh. "You think I want your money?"

He shrugged. "You're the one who sued me for child support."

"For *them*," she snapped. "Not for me. My God, you're incredible. Because I asked for child support you believe that means I'd be willing to be bought off?"

He shrugged, not letting her see that he was pleased at her reaction, if surprised. Not many people would have turned down a quarter of a million dollars without at least thinking about it first.

"You rich guys are all alike. The world runs on money. Well, maybe in your universe, but not here in reality. I want nothing from you. I make my own way and I always have. My business is exactly that—*my* business."

"Your business," he argued as he slowly pushed himself to his feet to face her across the kitchen table, "became mine when you became the guardian of *my* children."

He'd let her rant and rage, but she was going to understand this if he had to repeat himself ten times a day. "Those kids are what concern me. *My* children. Not yours."

She snorted. "You were the sperm donor. You're not a father."

Everything in him went still. Her words, practically spat at him, hung in the air between them like an ugly smear. "You don't get to say that to me," he said, his voice low and hard. "You know what Jackie and your sister did to me. You know the truth."

She gritted her teeth, pulling in a breath with a soft hiss. "Fine. You're right. About that. I shouldn't have said it. But you're not right about everything else. I don't want anything from you, Connor."

"Then you're the first woman I've ever met who didn't have an agenda. What're the odds on that?"

"What are you talking about?" Anger shifted to confusion.

"Every woman I've ever known has tried to use me— my name, my money, my family." His ego took a slight beating at the admission, but he was going to let her know from the jump just who was in charge here. "You think you've got issues with rich guys? Well, how would you like it if everyone you've ever known approached you with their hand out at one point or another? Jackie," he continued, "was the only woman who didn't try to use me in some way." A hard lump settled in his throat as he admitted tightly, "And in the end, she—and your sister—used me, too."

He hadn't meant to go that deeply into his own life. This was about Dina, the failing business she depended on and the welfare of the triplets.

It was a second or two before she spoke again. "Well, I'm not them."

"Yeah, you turned down the money. That's something. But," he added, tipping his head to one side as he studied her, "maybe you're just holding out for more." He didn't really believe that, but he felt a small slice of satisfaction when her eyes narrowed.

"I think you should go."

"Not gonna happen," Con told her. He glanced at the babies, who were now staring at the two of them with tiny worried frowns creasing each of their faces. Deliberately, Connor dialed back on the anger churning inside him. He wasn't going to traumatize his kids. "I'll tell you what is going to happen, though. You and the triplets are moving to my house. Starting today."

"You've got to be kidding."

"Nope. Dead serious." He planted both hands on the table and leaned toward her. "I'm not going to disappear from my kids' lives. I'm not going to be the last one you think of when you need backup to take care of them. And most importantly, I'm not going to try to sleep on that torture rack you call a couch again."

"You can't just decide something like this and expect me to go along—"

"Did you or did you not *just* say that the babies would always be taken care of no matter what you had to do?"

"Yes," she snapped. "But I didn't mean *this*."

He held up one hand for silence, and damned if he didn't get it. Con figured she was too surprised to argue. "Your house is too small for all of us and you know it."

"You weren't invited to stay," she pointed out.

"I'm their father. They stay with me."

"I'm their guardian. They stay with me."

"There you go," he said. "Neither one of us is going to give on this, so my solution works best."

"Because you say so."

"Because your whole house is the size of my closet." He pushed off the table and folded his arms across his chest. "You won't be bought off—which I admire, by the way."

"Wow." She tipped her head to one side and gave him a look that should have set fire to his hair. "Thanks."

He ignored the sarcasm. "You want the kids. So do I. The answer is, we both stay with them. We can't do that here, so my house is the logical move."

"Logical. That's all this is about?"

"What else?"

"And this new living situation," she said. "How would it affect us?"

"You're talking about the kiss last night?"

"No, I'm talking about what you might expect after the kiss last night."

A little insulted at the notion that he would maneuver her and the kids to his house as a way of forcing her into his bed, Connor frowned at her. "Relax. You'll have your own suite. I don't need to trick women into my bed. Or force them. They come willingly enough."

If she gritted her teeth any harder, her jaw might snap.

"I won't," she finally said and those two words, along with the situation, tugged a smile at the corner of his mouth.

"Yeah, I seem to remember you kissing me back last night."

"A minor bump in the road."

"Yeah we'll see about that."

"Trust me on this," she said, eyes flashing. "I won't be one of the legions of women who have rolled out of your bed."

"Don't paint yourself into a corner," Connor said. "Or make vows you'll just have to take back later."

"That won't happen."

"But the move will," he told her flatly and waited for her response.

She looked at the kids, each of them with banana smooshed across their tiny features. He could see her heart in her eyes as she looked at those children, and he knew the moment she made the decision to go along with his plan.

"Fine," she said tightly. "We'll come. *Temporarily.*"

"What's your definition of temporary?"

"I guess we'll find out, won't we?"

One eyebrow lifted. Once those triplets were in his house, they wouldn't be leaving again. Whether or not Dina stayed with them would be up to her. But one thing Con was sure of, in spite of her denials, was that before whatever this was between them ended, he would have her in his bed.

Six

"This is a mistake."

Dina's grandmother looked up from packing the babies' clothes and clucked her tongue. "That is not the right attitude to take."

"What other one is there?" Dina's insides were churning and she had a pounding headache. No doubt caused by last night's sleeplessness, the argument with Connor and now this hurried move that she was sure was going to turn into a disaster. "Living with Connor King? Even temporarily? Bad move. I can feel it."

Actually, what she felt was worry. Ever since he'd kissed her, she'd felt herself teetering on a shaky ledge. Moving into his house, onto his turf, sleeping in a room close to his…no way was this going to end well. Especially because as infuriating as the man was, as frustrating to deal with, he was also way too tempting.

And that wasn't even taking the triplets into consideration. He was getting the babies into—for lack of a better phrase—his possession. Surely that was going to mean something if he really did sue for custody. Any judge in the world would leave the babies in a palatial home cared for by a billionaire who could afford an army of nannies rather than with a nearly broke caterer living in a rented bungalow that was too small for one, let alone *four*, people.

"Oh, God."

Her grandmother did the tongue clucking thing again and Dina winced. "This is an opportunity for you to get to know the father of the children you love," the older woman said. "Use it. Learn what you can."

"You mean to use against him later?" She tapped her finger against her chin as she considered it. Dina couldn't risk Connor taking too much of the upper hand. As it was, she'd be living at his house, sharing the kids with him and reluctantly giving him a greater standing in the custody issue. She had to go into this ready to defend herself if need be.

"No," her grandmother said with a sigh. "I mean, get to know him. The two of you are now linked through these children. You will be a part of each other's lives always. Isn't it smart to know the person rather than to assume the worst and act on it?"

Dina groaned and plopped onto the bed, hands in her lap. "I hate it when you're rational."

The older woman chuckled and went back to folding tiny T-shirts and pants. "You don't want to admit he's right, either, do you?"

"He's not right. About what?"

"About this house. It is much too small for you and

three growing babies. You know this, Dina. You just don't want it thrown in your face."

True. The bungalow felt stifling most of the time. She had rented it three years ago for herself as a stepping-stone. A way to save money—since the rent then was reasonable—so she could save to buy her own place. With her business doing well, it wouldn't have taken her long to afford a nice condo somewhere. She'd built up a savings account, opened the catering company and was sure that all of her plans were going to sail on nicely.

But then the babies came, the rent went up, her business went down and she'd been pretty much stuck here. When Connor had said that her business was sinking and taking her dreams of a restaurant along with it, he'd really hit the nail on the head.

Maybe her grandmother was right. She would still have to pay rent on this house while living with Connor, just to keep her own place to run to when his plan was shot out of the sky. But everything else could work in her favor. Bills for diapers, food, babysitting wouldn't mount because she would be at his place. Maybe she could start saving again and begin to rebuild her nearly empty savings account.

"Fine. We'll go. We'll stay. For a while."

"Good. And you'll do this with a positive attitude."

"Oh, I'm positive this is all going to blow up in my face. Does that count?"

"No, it does not," her grandmother said, then asked, "What is this really about, *nieta*?"

Frowning, Dina picked at a splotch of dried baby food on the hem of her white shorts. "Connor King is over-powering," she finally said, her voice little more than a whisper of complaint. "He's gorgeous, he's pushy, he's rich."

"And you worry because of your mother."

Dina looked at her grandmother, apology in her eyes. Whatever kind of mom Helen had been to Dina, she had also been Angelica's daughter, and Dina felt guilty for reminding her grandmother of her loss. "I'm sorry. But you saw what happened to Mom, too. She would get involved with men who were larger-than-life and then she'd slowly crumble to whatever they wanted. She was lost, trying to be something she wasn't."

Sighing heavily, Angelica took a seat beside Dina, reached out and squeezed her hand. "I loved your mother," she said, "but she was not a strong woman. She had doubts about who she was, always. My daughter looked to men for the answer rather than to herself, and that was her mistake. Her fault. It's not yours."

Dina looked into her grandmother's eyes.

"You worry for nothing," her grandmother said softly. "You have a strength she never had, your mother. You are confident where she was hesitant. Strength in a man is not a bad thing. It is only weakness that can be devoured by strength. You have none."

Dina would like to believe that, but her confidence level was at an all-time low at the moment. Living with Connor, being around him nonstop, was going to be the kind of temptation she had always avoided. And that knowledge only made her feel even more uneasy about this whole thing.

"Now," her grandmother said as she stood up, "help me finish packing for the *niños*. It's time to face your fear and conquer it."

"Right. Conquer my fear." Dina stood up, too, and

looked at the pile of baby clothes still waiting to be folded. She had a feeling, though, as she started working again, that Connor King wasn't an easy man to conquer.

Of course his house was amazing. Set amid lush gardens and heavy greenery, it was a ranch-style home built of brick and stone and glass and looked as though it had simply grown organically where it stood.

Dina was speechless from the moment she entered through the double front doors. Polished oak floors, beautiful furnishings from the gleaming tables to the paintings on the taupe-painted walls to the gray marble fireplace that dominated one wall of the massive great room. It was there they settled the kids down to play and that Dina could take a moment to admire the room. Overstuffed furniture stood in silent invitation to curl up and relax. Books and magazines were stacked on the oak tables and a set of French doors opened onto a stone patio that fed down into a green lawn overlooking the ocean. One entire wall was glass, providing a view that was simply breathtaking, especially at the moment, with sunset spilling across the sea in a path of gold and red and staining the sky in shades of rose and gold and violet.

She did a slow turn, taking it all in and silently wishing she didn't feel like a peasant invited to the castle. The whole house smelled like fresh flowers and lemon polish. And though she hated to admit it, her entire bungalow would fit nicely into the great room.

The kids were at her feet, spread out on a wide rug that probably cost more than her car, with toys that were so new, she and Connor had had to pry them out of their packaging. Two nut-brown leather couches faced each other across a wide coffee table of distressed wood. Club chairs in varying shades of green and blue were scattered around the wide room in conversational groups and the wall of glass seemed to bring the outside in.

A housekeeper named Louise, a woman of about fifty, with graying dark hair and bright, curious blue eyes, had brought out tall glasses of iced tea along with a plate of cookies and three sippy cups of milk for the triplets. It was perfect, damn it.

"Think you'll be able to tough it out here?"

She turned to look at Connor, sprawled on one of the couches, looking exactly what he was...lord of the manor.

"Enjoying this, are you?"

"Being comfortable?" he asked. "After time spent on your couch? Oh, yeah."

She sighed because she couldn't really blame him. "Your house is beautiful."

He laughed shortly. "How much did that hurt?"

"A lot," Dina admitted. "I admit, I was hoping to find that you lived in some soulless, white everywhere modern nightmare—"

"Ooh, careful there. You just described my brother Colt's house."

"Really?"

He shrugged. "I never liked it. Felt cold to me, but he thought it looked clean. His wife and kids are currently dirtying it up for him."

"Right. Well, anyway. This house is beautiful, but you have to know that I feel like you maneuvered me into this move, and I don't like it."

"I did, and you don't have to." Connor straightened up in the chair, braced his elbows on his knees and slapped his hands together. "I want my kids, Dina. You come with them."

"For now," she said.

He lifted one shoulder. "Now's what we're dealing with, right?"

Yes, but what happened later? A week, two weeks, three? The longer they stayed in this house, the more solid footing Connor would have for a custody suit. And Dina wasn't an idiot. She knew he expected to take the kids from her. That thought made her heart ache, but a split second later, something clicked in her brain.

All along, she'd been thinking that Connor had the upper hand. And in a lot of ways, he did. But the reality of actually *living* with three babies who demanded plenty of attention was something he hadn't experienced yet. She smiled as she realized that staying here might actually work in her favor after all.

She knew that Connor had only been interested in being a part-time father before Elena and Jackie were killed. Now, it was his own sense of duty and honor—and the realization that he'd been lied to—that had him scrambling to take charge of the triplets.

But what if once he had what he wanted he didn't want it anymore? What if the day-to-day dealings with three babies showed him that he wasn't ready for fatherhood? This could turn out to be the best thing she could have done. Living here, letting him take charge of the kids, might just prove to him once and for all that the trips were better off with her.

She smiled to herself at the thought and relaxed for the first time since their kiss the night before.

"Why are you smiling?" he asked, voice colored with suspicion.

"No reason," she said. Meeting his gaze, she felt something inside her tremble and felt suddenly uncomfortable. But then, she wasn't comfortable with a lot lately. That kiss they'd shared had been overwhelming and the feelings it engendered were still with her. Along with anxiety. She'd never let a man get close enough to her to make her anxious about her feelings.

Looking across the room at Connor, she stared into his ice-blue eyes and knew that *this* man was dangerous. Not just to her guardianship of the babies, but to *her*.

"Louise has your room ready," he was saying. "It's upstairs, next to the babies' room. Mine's across the hall."

"Handy," she murmured.

"Isn't it?" He smiled and her stomach spun unsteadily.

"What's the matter, Dina?" he asked. "Don't trust yourself with me?"

Exactly, but she couldn't really admit to that.

"I think I can manage to restrain myself," she said, scooping Sadie off the floor and onto her hip.

"Wanna bet?" Connor stood up, grabbed the other two kids and held them while he looked into her eyes. A smile curved his mouth and something inside her flipped over in response.

Oh, yeah. This was not good.

A week later, Connor was a man on the edge.

Who would have guessed that three babies could take over a house in so little time? There were toys everywhere, forgotten sippy cups under the couch, and stains on half of his shirts. The three of them were a force of nature.

Connor was exhausted.

And it wasn't just the triplets wearing him down, either. It was the knowledge that Dina was just across the hall from him, every night. It was imagining her show-

ering, naked and wet, with water streaming along her
honey-colored skin. It was the images of her floating
through his mind, stretched out on the four-poster bed in
her room, wearing nothing more than a welcoming smile
as she held her arms out to him. It was remembering the
taste of her so well he still held her scent inside him.

The way she laughed, the way she smiled at the babies
or the way she held them, loved them. She was sparking
too many thoughts in his already tired brain and Connor
was sure that she somehow knew he was suffering—and
she was enjoying it.

Hell, Dina'd hardly lifted a finger for the kids since
they moved in. She'd taken a giant step back, telling him
that she was sure he wanted to get to know his children.
She left the bathing and feeding to him. She watched as
he chased them down every morning just to get them
dressed. And she laughed whenever one escaped him.

So Connor knew that she was expecting him to fail.
To surrender and say that he wasn't interested in full custody, that it was too much work or some other nonsense.
But she was going to be disappointed. He hadn't changed
his mind. If anything, his resolve had only strengthened
over the last week. His children belonged with him and
he was going to do whatever he had to do to make sure
that happened.

The question was, how to deal with Dina.

"She said no, didn't she?"

"What? Who? Oh. Yeah." Connor shook his head and
looked at Colt. Smoke from the barbecue on his patio
lifted into the sea wind and twisted into knots before
dissipating. The scent of cooking burgers filled the air.

A family barbecue had been Penny's idea. Colt's wife
had wanted to meet Dina and the kids.

"You mean to my offer of buying her off?" Grimly, he smiled at the memory of her outraged expression. "Yeah, she said no. And a few other things as well."

"Told you it wouldn't work," Colt said and took a drink of his beer.

"Thanks. *I told you so* is always so helpful to hear."

Colt ignored that. "So any ideas on where you go from here?"

"Plenty." He nodded, picked up the spatula and flipped the burgers on the grill. Grease dropped onto the coals and flames erupted.

"You should get a gas grill," Colt mused.

"I like charcoal," Con told him. "Anyway, Rafe and his crew are coming out next week to sketch out plans for the new nursery suite."

"And Dina knows you're doing this?"

"Not yet, but why should she care?"

"Oh, I don't know, because she thought moving in here was temporary and now you're making it permanent?" Colt's eyes narrowed on his twin. "What's going on in your head?"

"Plans. Okay," Con said, "I admit, it's a little tougher than I thought it would be, taking care of so many babies at once."

"As I remember it, you laughed your head off when it happened to me."

Connor ignored that. "My plans right now are to get to know my kids, to have the lawyer looking into custody and to get to Ireland."

"You taking Dina and the kids with you?"

"Why not?" He made it sound casual but the truth was, he had to go on this trip and didn't much care for the idea of being away from Dina and the babies for a

week. He refused to look at *why*. "Dina's got a passport
and I had the family lawyers arrange them for the babies. We'll go. Say hi to cousin Jefferson and his family
and check out Ashford Castle. Three, four days tops and
we're back in California." When his brother gave him a
knowing look, Con shook his head. "Don't make more
of this than there is. I'm taking the kids and Dina's part
of the package. That's all."

"Uh-huh." Colt took another drink of his beer, nodded
to where the women and kids were and said, "If you ask
me, she's quite a package all on her own."

"Nobody asked you," Connor snapped. Then he took
the burgers off the grill. "Time to eat."

"You didn't tell me you and your brother were identical twins," Dina said later after everyone had gone home
again.

"There are some differences," Connor said. "I'm the
good-looking one."

She laughed and realized that over the last week, she'd
become less anxious around him. Less wary. And that
should probably worry her. But at the moment she felt
too good to ruin her mood with anxiety.

With the triplets tucked into bed and the housekeeper
in her suite at the rear of the house, Connor and Dina
were alone. The patio was quiet and cool and the sound
of the ocean slamming into the cliffs below was rhyth-
mic, soothing. They sat on Adirondack chairs, each of
them holding a glass of wine.

"Colt's wife is great," she said. "Did you know she's
having the whole house redone?"

"Yeah. Our cousin Rafe at King Construction is madly
in love with her," Con said with a chuckle. "She's chang-

ing so much it's turned into a huge project that'll keep Rafe's crew busy for months."

"She pointed the house out to me earlier. The big white one that looks like a box with windows?" Dina had taken one look at the place and hated it. Penny had told her she'd felt much the same way when she first saw it. But she was having Spanish revival style added to the basic box and by the time she was finished, Dina was willing to bet that the house would be beautiful. "Penny also told me that Rafe was going to be taking a break from working on her house long enough to do a job for you."

"Told you that, did she?" He turned his head and looked at her, and in the moonlight, his blue eyes shone.

"You're building a suite for the babies but you didn't tell me?" When Penny brought it up, Dina had felt a quick jolt of panic. Adding onto a home was a permanent thing. To Connor's mind, this wasn't temporary at all.

"I was going to," he said, voice quiet and almost lost in the sigh of the waves below.

"You're really going to sue for custody, aren't you?"

He sat forward. "I never made a secret of the fact that I want my kids, Dina."

"I know," she said, shifting her gaze to where a full moon hung in a black sky and slanted silver light on the sea. "The problem is, I want them, too, Connor."

He stood up and pulled her to her feet. She was barefoot and the stone patio was damp and cold, seeping into her bones. With his hands on her upper arms, holding her in place, he looked down into her eyes and Dina felt that tremble of something wild and dangerous rise up inside her again.

"You don't want to fight me for them, Dina," he said. "You would lose."

"If I don't fight, I've lost already," she pointed out and congratulated herself on keeping her voice steady and even despite the insistent tremble she felt within.

The wind sighed past them, briefly enfolding them in a chilly embrace. Dina's hair flew across her eyes and Connor tugged it free, rubbing the silky strands between his thumb and fingers.

"We don't have to be enemies," he whispered. "We can find a way to work together on this."

"I don't see how," she said, staring into those blue eyes that only seemed to shine more brightly in the darkness.

"This is a start," he murmured and kissed her again.

Dina melted against him, plying her body along his as he pulled her in more tightly, pressing her to him closely enough that she felt the hard proof of what he wanted. Her insides churned, her heartbeat quickened and her mind went blessedly blank.

Her entire life had been spent trying to avoid the kind of feelings she was right now surrendering to. If she thought about what she was doing, she'd have to stop. Have to be rational. Logical. Clearheaded.

So she didn't think.

Dina gave her emotions free rein and let herself wallow in the amazing sensation of being held and kissed by a man who could turn her knees to water with a single look. She had known that one kiss would never be enough.

And when Connor pulled back, breaking contact, she knew that two kisses wouldn't be enough, either.

She was heading down a road she'd never intended to travel. But turning back simply wasn't an option now.

He cupped her cheek in his palm and smiled down at her. Dina's only consolation in all of this was that he looked as shaken as she felt. "What're we doing, Connor?"

"Right now?" He grinned, lifted her chin and planted a quick, hard kiss on her mouth. "We're saying goodnight while I'm still enough of a gentleman to let you walk away from me."

"That's not what I meant."

"I know," he said and stepped back and away from her. "Dina, I want you more than I've ever wanted anyone before, so I'm giving you fair warning. Leave now, or wake up in my bed."

Heat pooled in her center and her breath came just a little bit quicker. "I'm not sleeping with you, Connor."

"You're right about that, anyway," he said wryly. "Sleeping wasn't what I had in mind."

More heat flared until Dina felt as if she might simply spontaneously combust right there on the patio. Funny, all it took was warning her away from him to make her want him even more. How twisted was that?

"Connor—"

"Do us both a favor and go to bed, okay?" He scrubbed one hand across the back of his neck, then let his hand fall to his side.

"Fine. I'm going." She hadn't taken more than a few steps, though, when his voice stopped her.

"Oh, yeah. We'll be going to Ireland in a few days, if there's anything you need to take care of before we go."

"*Ireland?*"

Seven

Dina was being treated like a princess.

And she felt like a fraud.

For heaven's sake, she'd been whooshed through security, bypassing the thousands of people lined up at the other terminals, in favor of the charter jet area that was practically empty in comparison. That's when she discovered that flying on a KingJet was a far different experience than flying coach on a regular airliner.

The KingJet boasted comfy leather seats, a full bar and three cribs bolted to the floor to accommodate sleeping triplets. There was room to wander around and a bathroom—complete with shower—that was as luxurious as the rest of the plane. During the long flight to Ireland she'd relaxed by watching movies on a big-screen TV while Connor buried himself in work.

Once they landed, they were all once again hustled

through customs without having to wait like every other human being on the planet and ushered to a limousine complete with a liveried driver. The ride from Shannon airport to Ashford Castle took an hour and a half, but Dina was so busy with the triplets and admiring the view out the windows, she hardly noticed time passing.

Just the day before, she had been at home, scrambling for work—and now she was in Europe. Sadly, she hadn't had to do much in preparation for this trip. She had no immediate jobs lined up and so no reason to tell Connor she couldn't go with him. And now, as the beautiful countryside streamed past the car windows, she was glad for that.

Connor had been in Ireland before and enjoyed playing tour guide. "In a day or two, we'll drive over to Cong and take the kids for a walk through the village."

"Okay," she said, smiling. "What's Cong?"

He laughed. "Just a really beautiful village in Ireland, but they filmed *The Quiet Man* there. You know, the John Wayne movie?"

"I love that old movie," Dina said.

"Yeah, me, too. They've got a statue in the village commemorating the film, too. Plus, you can visit a perfect replica of the cottage they used. There's nice shops, some good restaurants and great pubs. You'll like it."

She was sure she would. What she wasn't sure of was why Connor cared if she was having a good time or not. But that question went unanswered as the limousine turned in to a long, graveled drive at the end of which the castle waited.

Once the car stopped, Dina stepped out and right into a fairy tale.

The castle was amazing. Weathered gray stone, trail-

ing ivy, glorious flower beds in vivid colors, forests and
a long, winding drive. There was a fountain in the center of the yard and a lake spread out in front of the castle, where sunlight glinted off the surface like handfuls
of diamonds.

Dina stood in one spot and did a slow turn, trying to
take everything in and failing. It would take months to
appreciate the whole picture. She had never seen so many
different shades of green, though. Standing there, it was
like being inside an emerald and watching sunlight play
among the shadows—cool and warm at the same time.

"It's a rare day for Ireland in June," Connor was saying. "Usually the skies are gray and the wind is cold and
generally it's raining. The sun must be shining today
just for you."

She laughed, delighted at the thought, even though it
was ridiculous. Then she shook her head and, speechless,
stared at the castle itself, from the ground all the way up
to the battlements, where she guessed ghosts still walked.

"You like it?"

"Oh, I really do," she admitted.

"It's the oldest castle in Ireland," he said, "and that's
saying something. I think it dates back to twelve hundred something."

"And it's still here," she mused, and her fingers itched
to touch the gray stone, to feel it hum with history and the
memories of everyone who'd ever been here. Smiling to
herself at the silly thought, she turned to look at Connor.
"It's incredible. I've never seen anything so beautiful."

He stared at her for a second or two then said, "Yeah.
Just what I was thinking."

Dina didn't even know how to respond to that and
thankfully, she didn't have to. A small crowd of peo-

ple rushed from the castle down the drive to the car. A short man in a sharp black suit and carefully tended hair walked directly to Connor and held his hand out.

"Mr. King," he said, in a voice brushed with a lovely accent. "So good to have you back again. We've your usual suite prepared for you."

"Thank you, Sean," Connor said, shaking the man's hand. "Dina, this is Sean Flannery, the castle manager."

"Nice to meet you."

"And you, madam," Sean said, taking her hand in a firm grip before turning back to Connor. "We've also taken care of your special requirements. The extra bedroom is equipped for your triplets, and may I add my congratulations to you and your lovely wife."

Dina blinked, surprised. Then she realized she shouldn't have been. Why wouldn't the hotel staff assume she and Connor were married? They were traveling with triplets, after all.

"Oh, thank you, but—"

Connor dropped one arm around her shoulders. "My wife's tired from the flight, Sean, so if you don't mind, I'd like to get us checked in right away."

"Certainly." He waved a hand and suddenly the throng of hotel employees with him descended on the limo, taking luggage out of the trunk and hurrying toward the arched stone doorway.

Dina gave Connor a look, but he shook his head as if to say *later*, so she let it go. Instead, she turned back to the limo and leaned inside. She unhooked the babies from their car seats and one at a time, she handed the kids out to Connor, who corralled them on the pristine lawn. But the triplets had been trapped for too long and refused to stand still. The three of them took off in different directions, toddling unsteadily across the grass, squealing and babbling as they went.

"We should catch them before they ruin the flower beds or fall into the fountain—"

"They're fine," Connor said, watching the three of them with a soft smile on his face. "Just exploring."

"Uh-huh." She glanced back at the noble facade of the castle and could only imagine the luxurious furnishings inside. With that thought came the worry of just what three curious babies could do to elegant accommodations. "Maybe we should have found a smaller hotel. Triplets? Here?"

"If you'll pardon me, Mrs. King," Sean said with a smile and a wink, "you're not to worry about a thing. This is Ireland. Children are welcome everywhere."

With those words, she felt more than welcome, and nearly relaxed. Until she saw Sadie pulling flowers up and had to run to catch the little girl before she did too much damage. Connor ran after the boys at the same time and while the Irish wind blew all around them, they worked as a team to gather the babies.

By the time they were settled in their palatial suite and had ordered room service dinner, the trips were ready for bed. Using teamwork, Connor and Dina got all three of them bathed and tucked in, then Connor poured two glasses of wine and they collapsed into lush green velvet wing-back chairs in the luxurious living room.

Through the wide windows that overlooked what she'd learned was Lough Corrib, Dina saw the twilight sky and the tips of the trees guarding the castle dancing in the wind. Still watching the magical scene outside, she took a sip of her wine and said, "The manager seems to know you very well. You even have your usual suite."

"I stay here when I visit my cousin Jefferson and his family." He eased back into the cushy armchair. "Maura's sheep farm is only a half hour away, and the castle is comfortable."

She laughed a little. "Comfortable? It's...I don't even have a word for it." Shaking her head, Dina said, "I've never been anywhere even remotely like it."

He stretched his legs out in front of him and crossed his feet at the ankles. "Wait until you see it at night with the moonlight on the lake. Pretty spectacular. Tomorrow, we can take the triplets down to the lake, let them throw rocks..."

"Or fall in and go swimming?"

"We'll be with them. But that's a good question. Have they taken swimming lessons yet?" he asked.

"No," she said, studying the gold-colored wine in her glass. "Elena was going to take them this summer, but—"

He frowned, took a small sip of his own wine and said, "We'll have to do it instead. My cousin Rafe is going to install a fence around my pool, but swimming lessons are pretty much life or death for kids, don't you think?"

"I agree."

"Good." He gave her a fast smile that resonated inside her with a heat she really didn't want to acknowledge. "I'll arrange for a private instructor to come to the house starting next month."

"I don't know that we'll still be at your house next month," she said.

"Oh, I think we can count on it." He tipped his head to one side and stared at her for a long moment or two.

"Connor..." He wasn't treating their move to his house as if it were temporary, but that was how she *had* to think of it. No matter what it felt like occasionally, she and

Connor and the trips weren't a family. They were…more like survivors of a shipwreck huddled together in what, at the moment, was a pretty fabulous lifeboat.

She had to make him see that she couldn't stay indefinitely at his house. But what could she say? She was too nervous to stay at his place? She didn't trust herself around him? Oh, a man that sure of himself really didn't need to hear anything like that. Muttering under her breath, she took a sip of her wine.

"What was that?"

"Nothing," she said. "So what are we doing here in Ireland, exactly?"

His mouth quirked as if he knew she was desperately trying to change the subject. "Well, I told you I've stayed here at the castle before, but this time I'll be talking with management, gathering information about what kind of activities they offer families and in general seeing if Ashford Castle would be a good fit for our family adventure company."

"I can't imagine anyone *not* enjoying staying here."

"Oh, it's beautiful," he agreed, shifting his gaze around the room, "but will it be enough to qualify as a family adventure? We'll see."

"Maybe it doesn't have to be so much about adventure as it does a family spending time together in an amazing place," she said. "I know the castle itself would be enough to capture the imagination of any child. They'd picture themselves as knights and princesses…"

He nodded. "You might be right about that. My brothers and I would have loved this place when we were kids."

Several seconds of silence passed before he asked,

"Did you see much of the triplets before they came to live with you?"

"What?" The change of subject threw her for a moment.

He stared into his wine, then slowly lifted his gaze to hers. "The babies. Did you see much of them before Jackie and Elena died?"

"Not a lot, because they were living in San Francisco," she said quietly, sensing the shift in his mood to contemplative, "but they came to visit and I went to see them a few times."

"What were they like?" His voice was so soft, it was almost as if he regretted asking the question at all. "The babies, I mean."

Looking at him, Dina felt a twist of sympathy. Over the last week or so, he'd become so involved with the triplets. She'd stopped expecting him to give up and walk away. The man would never turn his back on those children and he was doing more and more to convince Dina that he was actually *enjoying* being a father.

Bottom line was, Connor was changing his home, his world, to accommodate them and he had been cheated out of knowing them for the first year of their lives. Yes, cheated, she thought and sent a disgusted thought toward her sister, wherever she might be. Jackie and Elena had been wrong to keep the kids from him. Wrong to leave town and run rather than share the children with the man who had helped to create them. And if Dina had known the truth, she would have told Connor herself.

So maybe, she thought, she was wrong to fight him so hard on the kids now. But what choice did she have, really? She couldn't lose the triplets. Not even to their father. It would be like tearing her own heart out. He was watching her, waiting for to speak, to tell him about the children he hardly knew. She took a breath and said, "The babies were always so cute. But oh, boy, were they tiny when they were born."

A wistful smile curved his mouth as he tried to picture it. "I bet Jackie was afraid to pick them up."

"She was," Dina said with a laugh. "For a while, but she got over it because Elena insisted."

"What kind of mom was she? Jackie?"

"A little crazy. Fun." Dina smiled at the memories and tried to make them feel real for Connor. "Elena was the one with the schedule. She wrote everything down. What time the trips ate, napped, play time, bath time. My sister loved schedules." Now it was her turn to be wistful. Only three months since she'd lost her big sister and Dina missed her. "But Jackie was fun. As the kids got older, she would dress up to read them bedtime stories. She bought them all miniature baseball bats so they'd be ready to play as soon as they could walk…"

"Sounds like Jacks. She used to play shortstop. She was really good, too." His smile faded into a thoughtful frown.

Twilight crept into the luxuriously appointed room, and shadows lengthened. It felt intimate, sitting here in the half light with Connor, sharing memories with him so that he could hold the images in his mind. But, she realized suddenly, she could do better.

Reaching to the table beside her, she turned on a lamp that sent shards of light glancing off its carved crystal base. He scowled a little at the sudden brightness, but Dina ignored that and picked up her purse. Pulling her phone free, she turned it on, went to the gallery and asked, "Would you like to see pictures?"

His eyes flashed with interest and a warm smile curved his mouth. "Are you serious?"

She answered the smile with one of her own, then held her phone out to him. "I never delete anything," she said wryly, "so there are photos of them from newborn on."

He was already looking at the pictures, swiping his finger across the screen to look at more.

"Some of them I took, others Elena emailed to me."

He laughed.

"What?"

Connor looked up at her, a mixture of amusement and regret in his eyes. "This picture. Last Christmas, I guess."

Dina knew which photo he was talking about, but she went to him anyway, knelt at his side on the thick rug and looked at the phone screen. Three babies, dressed in candy-cane-striped footie jammies, each of them with a Santa hat on their heads and tiny white beards on their faces.

Still laughing, Connor asked, "Even Sadie had a beard?"

Dina smiled at the memory. She'd been at her sister's house when the two women took that picture to use as their Christmas card. "Jackie didn't want Sadie to feel left out," she said quietly.

"Sounds like her," he agreed. Slowly, he flipped through the rest of the pictures, not speaking again.

Dina stayed where she was, watching—his expressions, not the phone screen. Every emotion he felt flickered over his face, shining in his eyes, curving his mouth. On a too-small screen, he watched his children change and grow and it was clear that those pictures touched something inside him. When he'd finally come to the end—she really did need to delete at least some of those pictures—he handed her the phone.

"I missed so much already."

"You didn't know, Connor."

"Doesn't change anything." He turned his head to look at her. His eyes shone with sadness, but a glint of determination was there, too, and Dina braced herself for what he might say next.

"I won't miss any more time with my children, Dina."

Her hand closed around her phone and held it tightly. Wow, just a couple of minutes ago, she'd been feeling bad for him, taking his side against the memory of her own sister. But looking into his eyes now, she saw that *this* man didn't need her sympathy. "Meaning?"

"Meaning," he said quietly, "I'll never get back their first Christmas. They got their first teeth, took their first steps, all without me even knowing of their existence."

"I know, Connor and it's terrible, but—"

He shifted in his chair, cupped her chin in his palm and lifted her face to his. "You and me, Dina, we're going to have to come to an understanding."

"What kind of understanding?"

"Well, that's the question, isn't it?" he whispered. "I know what kind I'm interested in. I guess all we need is for you to decide for yourself what it is you want here."

Oh, she knew what she *wanted*. Dina just didn't know if getting what she wanted would make things better… or worse.

Watching Connor with his family was a revelation. Oh, she knew he was close to his twin—why wouldn't he be? But Jefferson King was a cousin and yet he and Connor seemed as close as brothers. Obviously, family was vastly important not only to Connor but to the Kings in general. That acknowledgement underscored what she'd felt only the night before. As his children, the triplets weren't something Connor would risk losing.

"Lovely, aren't they?"

Dina glanced at Maura King. The woman was short and gorgeous, in spite of her heavy rubber boots, and the oversize jacket she wore over a thick red knit sweater. June in Ireland, just as Connor had told her, meant clouds, wind, cold and spatters of rain.

They'd gone shopping in the village of Craic only that morning, buying the triplets warmer clothing, since a California wardrobe didn't prepare anyone for the damp chill. Ireland was beautiful and wild in a way that California never could be, and Dina loved it already.

Maura King had been a sheep farmer when Jefferson, scouting a location for one of the movies King Studios made, met her for the first time. Since she still ran her farm and Jefferson worked from the manor house, Dina assumed that marrying one of the wealthiest men in the world hadn't changed Maura Donohue King much.

"Lovely?" Dina repeated, glancing back to where Connor, Jefferson and six children—Maura and Jefferson had three of their own and another on the way—raced madly around the yard alongside a galloping black-and-gray Irish wolfhound named King. Dina had thought his name to be an odd choice, but Maura had explained that she'd gotten the wolfhound when she and Jefferson were on the outs and that she had named the dog after him because, she said, like Jefferson, the dog was a "son of a bitch."

The sheer size of the dog had intimidated Dina at first. She'd never seen such a big animal. But as Maura promised, a wolfhound was the original gentle giant. In no time at all, the triplets were crawling across the big dog, pulling his ears and stepping on his huge feet, and King never made a sound. Rather, he acted like a nanny, herding the kids back into the center of things when they wandered too far on their own.

"Yeah," Dina said, smiling at Connor's hoot of laughter as Jefferson's oldest son, Jensen, sneaked up behind his father and gave him a swat. "I guess they are lovely. So's your home, by the way," she added, turning her face to look out across the pewter-colored waters of Lough Mask, spread out beneath gray skies.

Trees bent in the ever-present wind and tiny whitecaps formed on the lake's surface. Narrow roads lined with gorse bushes boasting tiny yellow flowers spilled through green fields dotted with rock walls like thread loosed from a spool. The farmhouse itself was big and old and behind it rose the Partry Mountains, looking like a purple smudge on the horizon.

"Thank you," Maura said, giving her house a quick glance over her shoulder. "I like it, too, just as it is, but Jefferson is forever adding this or changing that, until I'm never sure what I'll find when I come in from the fields."

"But you don't really mind."

"Not a'tall, but don't tell him I said that." She winked and smiled. "The man is too sure of himself already."

Dina laughed. "I think that's a King thing."

"Perhaps," Maura said, leaning on the fence that surrounded the front yard. "Since all of his brothers are exactly the same and the few cousins I've met as well. Still, I wouldn't change him for the world. I find I like a man who angers me as often as he attracts me."

"In that, Connor and Jefferson are alike," Dina mused,

thinking of the many arguments she and Connor had had in the short time they'd known each other. And yes, like Maura, Dina was attracted even when she was furious with the man.

"I've seen the way he looks at you and you at him." Maura smiled and tapped her fingers against the top rail on the fence.

Dina didn't even comment on that—what could she say? That it wasn't true? Hardly.

"And the children are sweet."

"They are. But so are yours," Dina said, turning to look at the kids as they raced around the yard in the sharp, cold wind.

Maura chuckled. "Wild heathens they are, and treasures, each and every one of them. Jensen was the first— he's four now—and then Julie came along a year or so later and then James."

Dina watched the kids playing and laughing and felt her heart turn over at the sight. How would it be, she wondered, to actually be a part of that group? Oh, she belonged, through the triplets. She was their aunt as well as their guardian and that would never end. But Maura, Jefferson and their children and Connor and the triplets were *family*, and that connection continued to elude Dina. It was simply ridiculous to wish to be more deeply involved with Connor when at the same time she was trying desperately to stay out of his bed just to protect her own heart.

Even more ridiculous to admit that up until she'd met Connor, she had instinctively avoided anything remotely resembling a real relationship. Memories of her mother's tumultuous life were too clear in Dina's mind to allow for anything else. And yet, somehow Connor had slipped past her defenses.

"And with three children, you're pregnant again," Dina said with a glance toward Maura's rounded belly.

"My Jefferson is mad for children, wants as many as we can handle." Maura ran one hand over her belly as if soothing the restive child within. "And as I agree and find I love being a mother more every day, I'm thrilled to be having another. Even if it does mean Jefferson is adding another wing onto the house, crazy man that he is."

Dina laughed but felt a tug of envy for the relationship Maura and Jefferson shared. He ran his movie studio from right here with the occasional trip to the States. Maura remained her own person and operated her sheep farm just as she always had, and yet the two of them together were a team that was only enhanced by the kids they shared. Who wouldn't be envious?

Dina's gaze locked on Connor, pretend wrestling with Jefferson and the kids. Squeals of laughter from the children were swept up by the cold Irish wind and carried away like dreams. She smiled to herself and if that smile was a little wistful, who could blame her?

"King men are difficult even at the best of times," Maura told her suddenly, as if deciding to skip the polite niceties and just get to the meat of the matter. "But I can tell you from personal experience that they're worth the trouble."

"It's not like that with us, Maura," Dina said quickly.

Maura laughed. "Ah, yes. I remember fighting it myself. Jefferson was forever tossing his money about, waving it in my face. Did you know that he actually bought me a lorry without even speaking to me about it?" Shaking her head as she remembered, she continued. "Red it was, and as shiny as a promise, and though I shouted and raged at him for buying the bloody thing, I fell in love with it the moment I saw it. I still drive it now and it's as lovely as ever it was."

Dina laughed and shook her head. "He bought you a truck."

"Aye. Because he said I needed it whether I wanted to admit it or not. And he was right, though I was loath to admit to it. My old beast was on its last wheels, so to speak. But that's who the Kings are, you see. They make a decision they feel is right and good luck to you trying to convince them otherwise."

"I don't like being managed," Dina said.

"And who does? But that's not saying you can't do some managing of your own, is it?"

Dina smiled at the other woman. "You know, I think you and I are going to be great friends."

"I feel it already," Maura said with a matching grin. "And, as Jefferson has decided that we must all fly to California next month to take the heathens to Disneyland before this one is born, I'll be seeing you again soon. You can tell me all about how the managing of Connor King is coming along."

Next month. Dina didn't even know if she'd still be at Connor's house in a month.

"Maybe we could all go to the amusement park together. That would be lovely." Maura turned her face into the wind. "I'll call my sister, Cara, and make sure she's available for it as well. As busy as she is, she does love to see the children when we're in the States."

"Cara." Dina thought about that for a moment. The sign at the front of Maura's farm still read Donohue

Sheep Farm, despite the fact that the owner was a King now. So…Cara Donohue. "Your sister is Cara Donohue?"

Maura's features lit up. "You've seen her films then?"

"I have. She's wonderful." And she'd had no idea that Hollywood's favorite young actress was related to the King family.

"She is that," Maura said proudly. "It was the film Jefferson shot here on the farm that gave her the big break. She'd done some soaps in London, but after this small film here, Jefferson signed her to do—"

"O'Malley's Bride," Dina finished for her.

"The very one." Maura practically beamed with pride. "She was nominated for best actress for the role. She didn't win, of course, but the nomination itself was a wonder."

This whole trip was a wonder, Dina told herself. Maura was kind and friendly, Jefferson was warm and funny, and Connor…she looked at him, and as if he felt her watching him, he caught her gaze and gave her the smile that made her knees weak and her insides nearly purr.

"Oh, yes," Maura whispered, giving her a little elbow nudge. "There's plenty there to be managed, Dina. Up to you, of course, but a King, as I said, is more than worth the trouble."

Whatever the two women had been talking about earlier had put Dina in an odd mood. Though she'd been patient with the triplets as always, it was as if her body was there, but her mind somewhere else. Back at the castle, with the babies asleep, Connor joined Dina at the open window in the living room. A cold wind rushed inside, but she made no move to shut it. Her long black hair lifted and twisted in that breeze and flew about her face in a dark halo. Her hands gripped the windowsill and her face was turned into the wind, the night.

"Are you all right?"

"I don't know," she said softly.

He took her arm and pulled her around to face him. Studying her eyes, he tried to read what she was thinking, feeling, but though those chocolate depths called to him as always, he couldn't make out what she was hiding from him. The only way to find out was to dig beneath the surface.

Exactly what he'd been aching to do for too long.

He'd never known this kind of overpowering desire. Usually when he wanted a woman, he had her. But for too long all he'd been able to do was ache for Dina. Most of the women he'd come across in his life had leapt at the chance to climb into his bed. The problem had always been getting them to leave again.

Naturally, Dina was different. And he liked that. In fact, everything about her appealed to him. Her gentleness with the babies, her willingness to stand up to him for what she believed was right—the fact that she didn't want anything from him except what he owed the babies. She had even been insulted at the thought of him buying her off. She was damned fascinating in every way and he hadn't expected that. Con wasn't interested in feeling anything other than the desire that pounded inside him. He wasn't interested in *depth*. Wasn't looking for forever. What he wanted was *her*.

"You're thinking," he said, in a quiet, teasing tone. "That can't be good for me."

Reluctantly, she smiled. "Might not be good for me, either," she admitted. "Look, Connor, I think we have to figure out what we're doing here. I can't continue to stay at your house with the trips indefinitely. I have a life and a business to run. I can't just walk away from that."

"Who's stopping you from running your business from my house?"

"That only solves one issue," she said, clearly frustrated. "I can't stay with you, Connor, just because you think it's more convenient."

"You'll be with me, Dina," he said, "because you won't lose the triplets and I'm not giving them up."

"So where does that leave us, exactly?" She shook her hair back from her face and looked up into his eyes. "Neither one of us is willing to give in, so we just live with a stalemate?"

He couldn't give her an answer because he didn't have one. On this trip, it had felt almost as if they were a family. He'd allowed the castle manager, Sean, to assume Con and Dina were married—he'd considered it expedient earlier, but maybe the truth was that he hadn't minded the assumption as much as he would have expected.

And that realization was staggering, so he put it aside to look at later. Maybe. Right now there was only one thing he was interested in and he was done waiting.

"Why worry about any of this tonight, Dina?"

"We have to—"

"Right now, all we have to do is this." He cupped her face in his palms, bent his head and touched his mouth to hers. Soft, gentle, barely a brush of lips to lips before he pulled back and looked down into her eyes.

"I want you, Dina," he said, his voice as quiet as his kiss. "I have from the first moment I saw you."

"I know," she whispered. "Me, too."

He smiled and bent his forehead to hers. The knots inside him loosened and his body went hard and ready in a heartbeat. "Then what're we waiting for?"

Eight

Taking her hand, Connor grabbed the baby monitor from a nearby table before stalking to his bedroom while Dina hurried to keep up. Once inside, he closed the door, set the monitor down and drew Dina into the circle of his arms. He indulged himself with a long, deep kiss, savoring the taste of her, the feel of her, the sweet surrender she offered to the fires burning between them.

Moonlight slanted through the windows and lay across her face and hair like molten silver. She shimmered with beauty that had haunted him from the first. His mouth went dry as he pulled back to fill his gaze with her.

The room was dark but for that pale wash of moonlight. A four-poster spindle bed took up most of the space but there were tables, chairs and a blue tiled hearth that lay dark and cold.

"This is probably a mistake," she said and Connor's heart stopped for a second.

"That mean you want to stop?" He'd stop if she'd changed her mind, but he was pretty sure it would kill him.

"No," she said with a small shake of her head.

"Thank God." They'd waited long enough. Too long. This tension between them had been building since that first day when she'd faced him down in her tiny kitchen. They'd been headed here, to this moment, ever since. Con knew she was right—this probably was a mistake—they still had so much to work out between them, sex would only complicate things. But he'd figure that out later. Right now, they'd waited long enough.

He backed her up to the bed, lifting the hem of her sweater to help her tug it off. Connor couldn't wait to get his hands on her. He wanted to feel her skin beneath his hands. Wanted to touch and explore every tempting curve he'd been dreaming about for days.

Her hands worked at his sweater just as feverishly, her eagerness feeding his own. And yet, even in the rush to get her naked, Connor felt a driving need to take his time, to savor this moment that had been so long coming.

Deliberately, he slowed things down, forcing himself to strangle the urge to toss her onto the bed and bury himself inside her. He unbuttoned her shirt and carefully slid it down her arms to drop to the floor. She shivered as she stood before him wearing only her bra and a pair of blue jeans.

"Are you cold?"

"No," she said. "The way I feel right now, I may never be cold again."

One corner of his mouth lifted. "Good. That's good."

He trailed his fingers down her sides, sliding over her rib cage, down to her abdomen and up again to the front clasp of the black bra that looked devastatingly sexy against her smooth, honey-colored skin.

He thumbed the clasp open and let her breasts spill into his hands. He cupped their weight and rubbed his thumbs across the tips of her hardened nipples. In response, she sucked in a gulp of air and swayed unsteadily. Connor knew how she felt. His insides were twisted together in heavy, hungry knots. He'd never known such overpowering desire for anyone. Never experienced such pleasure from a simple touch. Maybe it was because of the growing connection they shared because of the triplets. Maybe, he told himself, it was because they'd waited so long to satisfy their shared hunger. Maybe his own dreams were feeding the reactions scuttling through his body like skyrockets.

But the why didn't really matter. All that did matter now was her and the smooth, silky feel of her.

He bent his head to taste her, taking first one nipple, then the other into his mouth. Her breath raced in and out of her lungs. She arched into him, silently asking for more. His heartbeat galloped when she responded by lifting her hands to his shoulders and holding him to her with a nearly desperate grip.

But she couldn't keep him still, not when he wanted to explore all of her. He was a man on a mission now, with nothing more on his mind than fulfilling all of the fantasies he'd indulged in over the last week or more. He slid down her length, his hands moving to release the snap of her jeans and then the zipper. Slowly, he pushed the denim, along with the black panties they'd been hiding, down her legs, following their trail with his mouth.

Her legs went weak until she locked them in place. He pulled her jeans off, stroking every inch of her skin as he did, then he stood up again slowly, sliding his hands over her body, reveling in the sweet feel of her. This was so much more than he'd imagined it would be. Her desire fed his, fanning the flames within until he was a walking inferno, ready to combust.

When he straightened again, Con took her mouth in a hungry kiss while allowing his right hand to shift to the sweet spot between her thighs. A muffled groan tore from her throat when he touched her so intimately for the first time. Then she pulled him closer as their mouths fused and their tongues tangled in nearly frantic desperation.

She was hot and slick and so ready for him, Connor could hardly breathe. He tore his mouth from hers so he could look down into her passion-glazed eyes as he worked her body into a frenzy. His fingers stroked and delved deep. His thumb slid across that hard nubbin of sensation at her core until she whimpered with the crashing need consuming her.

His hand cupped the back of her neck, holding her steady as their gazes locked. She was helpless to hide her response from him and didn't try. Her hips rocked into his hand as he pushed her higher, faster. Caressing her inside and out, he drove her to the edge of completion then pulled her back, refusing to allow her to find release too quickly. He wanted…needed to keep touching her. To hear her sighs, her whispered pleas. He wanted to stare into her eyes and watch as passion flared.

Her hands curled into his upper arms and even through the fabric of his shirt, he felt that contact like match points, burning into his skin.

"Let go, Dina," he told her softly, unable to look away from her amazing eyes. Such fire. Such passion. All for him. "Stop fighting it and let go."

"Connor—" She gasped for breath, his name barely more than a strained whisper shuddering from her throat.

"Do it, Dina," he demanded and plunged two fingers into her heat.

She exploded. Her body shook, her hips pumped wildly against him, and she tossed her head back, crying out his name in a strangled gasp.

Before she had even stopped trembling, Connor reached down and threw back the dark red duvet, exposing crisp white sheets. He laid her down, stripped out of his own clothes and paused only long enough to grab a condom from the bedside table, rip open the package and sheathe himself before he joined her on the massive bed. She lifted her arms in welcome and he slid into the circle of her heat, her warmth, like a man who had been freezing for far too long.

She parted her thighs and took him inside her. He entered her in one long stroke, feeling her silky heat surround and envelop him. For one long, heart-stopping moment, he held perfectly still, savoring the sensations of finally being where he most wanted to be. Then her legs came up to wrap around his hips, pulling him deeper, closer. He moved within her, slowly at first, setting a rhythm she matched, even as her hands moved up and down his back, her short, trim nails scoring his skin, driving him on. His hips pistoned, his body claiming hers in an ancient blending of selves.

They moved as one, pushing each other toward a release that hung just out of reach. He kissed her again and again, their mouths taking and giving as their bod-

ies raced to completion. He felt the tremors of her release take her and when she tightened her grip on him
and shouted his name, he let go and joined her, submit-
ting to the inevitable as his soul shattered.

Dina held him long after the last aftershocks of what
could only be called a nine-point-five on the Richter
scale slowly faded away. She'd never known anything
like that. Hadn't even guessed that her body was capa-
ble of feeling so much. Oh, she wasn't a virgin, reacting
to the first experience of a male-driven orgasm. But in
a weird way, the fact that she'd had three previous lov-
ers only underlined the extraordinary truth of what had
just happened.

Until tonight, she would have said that sex was good
and orgasms were pretty nice. But those pitiful words
didn't come close to defining what had just happened
to her. With his every touch, Connor had set her body
and soul on fire. She'd felt him right down to her bones
and even they had trembled under his sensual onslaught.
Now, with his weight pressing down on her, she felt…
complete somehow, in a way she never had before.

And that's when it hit her. She loved Connor King.
Dina didn't know when it had started, or when she had
taken that last slippery slide into love, but it was here
now. She was sure of it. Oh, God, how clichéd was that?
Have incredible sex and assume you're in love?

She squeezed her eyes shut as her brain raced. This
wasn't just about the sex, her brain argued. It was about
everything else—the way he handled the triplets, his
loyalty to family, his willingness to include her, even
his stubbornness—and the amazing orgasms were pretty
much just the icing on an incredible cake. Yet another

part of her mind demanded to know how this was even possible. She'd known him about two weeks. It shouldn't have been feasible to love someone after such a short period of time. It was nuts to even think it, but this feeling she had was undeniable.

Opening her eyes again, she stared up at the ceiling as the irony of her situation sank in. For most of her life, Dina had avoided situations that could lead to love, and here she found herself loving the very man she'd been at odds with from the beginning. It had to be a cosmic joke at her expense.

But while she worried over the implications, she also couldn't help relishing the moment. Love. Whether it would eventually bring her joy or pain, she didn't know. Sliding her hands up and down Connor's back, she relished this moment, this realization, even though it terrified her. For right now, she was at an Irish castle, in bed with the man she loved, and she wasn't going to waste another second worrying about what tomorrow would bring.

There would be time enough to tangle her thoughts around trying to trust that a man could accept her as she was without expecting her to change and be what he preferred. Plus, there was the fact that the only thing holding her and Connor together was the triplets. If he got custody of those babies, he wouldn't need her anymore and she'd be gone. She knew that and hated it.

Oh, loving him was a tremendous blunder, but God help her, she didn't know how to correct that error now, when it was too late to turn back.

"Are you okay?" he asked, lifting his head to look down at her.

Could he sense what she was thinking? Feeling? No,

she told herself firmly. If he could he would be leaping off the bed and putting some distance between them. So she buried her newly realized emotions deep and kept her response light. "I'm *great*," she said, smiling into those ice-blue eyes.

He gave her a brief, hard kiss. "Me, too." He skimmed one hand over to cup her breast and she gulped. Amazingly enough, her body, hardly recovered from that first incredible round, was clearly ready to go again.

She felt him pulse inside her and knew he felt the same. "Connor—"

He shook his head, his smile gone, replaced by the stamp of fresh need on his features. "I want you again. And again. And again."

"We should probably talk about this—"

"Yeah, not really interested in talking." He eased away and off the bed. "Don't move," he ordered.

She didn't think she could move if she had to. Besides he was back a moment later. He grabbed a fresh condom, slid it on and was joining her in the bed an instant later.

"No more talk," he whispered, sitting on his heels, drawing her with him until she straddled his lap, holding his hard length deep inside her. Dina shook her hair back from her face, looked into his eyes as his hands settled on her hips and dismissed the notion of some awkward conversation. There would be plenty of time for that later.

She squirmed on top of him, twisting her hips, creating a delicious sort of friction that rekindled the fire still licking at them.

"Ride me, Dina. Take me to the edge and then jump off with me."

She nodded, breathless at the explosion of sensation rocketing through her. Moving on him, she set a blistering pace, helped along by his strong hands at her hips. The only sound in the room was their eager gasps and the good, healthy slap of skin on skin.

She took him deeper, higher than she would have thought possible, until Dina was convinced he was actually touching the tip of her heart. She moved her hands from his broad shoulders to cup his face and then she kissed him, parting his lips with her tongue, demanding entry. Demanding he give her all that he had and then just a little more.

He threaded the fingers of one hand through her long, thick hair and held her head in place while he gave her just what she needed. And this time, when their shared release crashed down on them, their mouths were fused and each swallowed the other's moans of indescribable pleasure.

When it was over, they stared at each other and Dina wished she could read what was in his mind, his heart. Did he feel anything for her beyond desire? Was there caring and affection, too? Could that turn to love if given enough time?

And would they have that time? This move to his house was temporary and she knew it. Now, especially, she couldn't continue to live with a man she loved knowing he didn't love her in return. Could she?

He bent his forehead to hers and fought to steady his breathing. Their eyes met and he smiled. "Give me a half hour and we can go again."

Since her body was still buzzing with the kind of pleasure she'd never known before, she liked that idea. "It's a deal," she said, still willing to put aside all of her recent revelations until she could be alone with the craziness now settling in to stay in her mind.

"You are definitely my kind of woman," Connor said, grinning now as he rubbed her nipples with his thumbs.

She sighed, loving that near electrical charge zipping through her system. "Keep that up and we'll never make your half-hour timeline," she warned.

"I'm willing to risk it," he said, dipping his head to plant his mouth at the pulse point at the base of her throat.

Dina tipped her head back to give him access and felt the deliciously slow build of excitement stirring in her again. "You're not playing fair."

He smiled against her skin and whispered, "I'm a King, honey. We always get what we want."

Her heart turned over. He wanted her. But for how long?

From across the room, the baby monitor erupted with a half cry that splintered the haze of passion as surely as hitting a light switch chased away darkness.

Sighing, Connor pulled back and looked at her. Smoothing her hair from her face with his fingertips, he said, "Duty calls."

Duty. Why had he chosen that word in particular? Were the triplets merely duty, in spite of the way he treated them? The way he acted when he was with them? Was *she* a duty? Or was she simply handy?

"Yeah," she said, shifting to move off of him as her thoughts darkened and doubts spilled through her veins like tar. "I should go take care of that before whoever it is wakes up the other two."

"No," he said, catching her hand as she moved to grab her clothes. "I'll take care of it. You don't have to do it all anymore, Dina. You've got me."

He pushed off the edge of the bed, pulled on his jeans but didn't bother buttoning the fly. He cupped her chin in his palm, tipped her face up and gave her a quick kiss followed by that half smile that always tugged at her heart. "I'll be back. Don't go anywhere."

She didn't. Dina sat on the edge of the rumpled bed and thought back to what he'd said before. *She had him.* Did she really?

A week later, they were back in Dana Point and Ireland was nothing but a great memory.

Connor grinned to himself as he walked up to the front door of his house. He'd never enjoyed a business trip more. Sure, he'd secured a new adventure for his and Colt's business, but it was more than that. It was spending time with his family—the triplets, Maura and Jefferson and their brood—and it was discovering just how good he and Dina were together.

He hadn't expected it, but maybe he should have. She was nothing like any other woman he'd ever known, so why would *sex* with her be ordinary? Instantly, his body went tight and hard and he wasn't even surprised. Simply the thought of Dina stirred the hunger that was always close at hand.

Connor opened the front door of his house and was hit by a wave of delicious scents pouring down the hall from the kitchen. Mexican food. And since his housekeeper, Louise, had never once cooked Mexican for him, he knew exactly who was at the stove. Smiling to himself, he followed the amazing aromas and pushed the kitchen door open. He stopped in the doorway, fixed his gaze on her and just enjoyed the show.

Dina's long black hair was pulled into a high ponytail at the back of her head. She was barefoot and wore a dark red T-shirt with faded, skintight cutoff denim shorts. Music drifted from the speakers overhead and she moved to the rhythm, dancing across the white and gray marble floor tiles. His gaze fixed on the sway of her hips and his mouth went dry.

They'd been back from Ireland for two days and she hadn't been in his bed since they left the castle. The hell of it was, he missed her. He couldn't remember a time when a woman had made such an impact on him that he actively missed being with her. Until Dina, women had been fleeting distractions.

She was different. He wanted her here. Now. Teeth clenched, he got a grip on his needs and took a single step into the room. "Smells great in here."

Dina shrieked, spun around and slapped one hand to the base of her throat. "You scared me."

"Sorry." He shrugged. "You didn't hear me come in." Glancing around the kitchen, his gaze swept across the familiar pale gray walls, red and white marble countertops and white cabinets. The room was big and he'd probably only seen it a handful of times since he'd moved into the house four years ago. This was Louise's territory and he didn't intrude on it.

"So where are the kids?"

"Louise is watching them upstairs," Dina said. "I had to make the appetizers for a cocktail party and she volunteered to babysit so I could work faster."

"So we don't get to eat any of this stuff?" His gaze slid across the trays stacked on the end of the counter and the big round table set against a bay window. Late-afternoon sun streamed through that window in golden shafts that cut through the room and sparkled off the stainless steel fridge.

"We get to eat this." She turned back to the stove and

lifted the lid off a tall soup pot to allow a cloud of steam to lift from the surface.

Connor took a deep breath and sighed. "That smells amazing. What is it?"

"Chicken tortilla soup," she said and let him peek into the pot before she slapped the lid back down on it. Her gaze met his and just for a second, he saw the same kind of desire he was feeling. And, as if she sensed what he was thinking, she cleared her throat, stepped back from him and busied herself with the trays of goodies she had prepared.

He walked over and stopped beside her, close enough that their arms brushed together. Connor heard her quick intake of breath and smiled to himself.

"So, what else do you have here?"

As she snapped the clear plastic lids on the trays, she said, "Mini chicken chimichangas, red-pepper-and-spinach quesadillas, shredded beef taquitos, cheese-stuffed jalapenos, and pulled pork miniburritos."

He snagged one of those before she put on the lid and he'd taken a bite before she had time to whirl on him and say, "Hey! That's for my client."

Connor groaned as flavors exploded in his mouth. Everything had looked great on the trays, but one taste told him that she was a damn artist with a stove. He could understand now why she wanted to open a restaurant. The woman was a *chef*.

Chewing slowly, he shook his head and looked at the half a burrito he still held. "That," he said with reverence in his tone, "is incredible."

She smiled, pleased at the compliment. "Thank you." Sighing, she said, "I've been cooking since early this morning and now that everything's done I've got to shower and change so I can deliver the food to my client."

Connor ate the last of his burrito and tried not to send a greedy glance at the covered trays. "Where's the cocktail party?"

"Long Beach," she said, turning away to stack the trays neatly. "So I've got to run. Now that you're back, you can take over for Louise. I'm sure she's more than ready for a break by now."

"Long Beach is, like, an hour from here," he said, not liking the thought of her having to drive alone all the way back after the party. It would probably be after midnight and if she drove down Pacific Coast Highway, there were plenty of dark stretches she'd have to pass through.

Frowning, he realized he was *worried* about her.

"Do you have someone working the party with you?" he asked.

"No," she said. "This is a small affair. I can handle it on my own."

"Maybe I should go with you," he blurted out, almost as surprised by the offer as she appeared to be.

Dina looked at him. "Why?"

Shrugging, he said, "I can help you carry those trays, for one. Help set up, drive you to and from…"

"What's going on with you?" Her dark brown eyes were fixed on his, gleaming with curiosity.

Good question, he thought. Even Connor wasn't sure why he was so drawn to her. Why being around her made him feel more alive. More…hell. Just *more*. After that week in Ireland with her, he'd found that he wanted to be around her all the damn time. To hear her laugh. To watch her with the kids. To have her turn to him with those big dark eyes open and shining with pleasure.

To reach across his bed and have her turn in to his arms. But he wasn't about to say all of that to her, so he went with the most immediate reason.

"I don't like the idea of you driving around so late by yourself, is all."

A slow, pleased smile curved her mouth just before she went up on her toes and planted a soft, quick kiss on his lips. "That is very sweet."

Now Connor frowned. He wasn't sweet. Ask anybody.

"Dina," he said, catching her hand in his as she started to walk past him. His insides were tangled up in a mess of sensations, emotions and thoughts he didn't want to explore. But there was one thing he had to say to her before she walked out of the room. One thing he wanted straightened out.

She looked down to where their hands were joined, then lifted her gaze to his again. "I can't talk now, Connor. I've got a job and I have to go do it."

He didn't let her go. Instead, he gave her hand a squeeze and held on. "Yeah. Another minute's not going to make that much difference."

"Okay. What is it?"

"Since we got back from Ireland, you've been staying in your own room."

"Yeah," she said, inhaling sharply, "I thought it would be best if we got back to reality."

"Reality sucks," he said, giving her hand a tug hard enough to pull her into him. He looked down into her eyes, let her see the need, the hunger in his. He lifted his free hand to cup her breast and smiled when she closed her eyes and sighed in response. Dragging his thumb across her nipple, he felt it harden even through her bra and the thin fabric of her shirt. "I want you, Dina. Right now, but I'll settle for tonight."

"Connor…" Whatever she was going to say changed as seconds ticked past with their gazes locked, their bodies pinned tightly together. She licked her lips, sending a zip of heat sliding through him.

"Okay," she said at last, reaching to cover his hand on her breast with her own. "Tonight."

"And then every night after," he said, knowing he was pushing and not giving a good damn. Having his hands on her again was both torture and delight.

"And every night after," she said softly, shaking her head as if she knew she was making a mistake but was determined to do it anyway. "This is crazy, you know that, right?"

"No. What's crazy is knowing what we have together and not having it."

She laughed shortly. "Still, not a good idea."

"Best idea since pizza," he countered.

"I guess we'll see." Reluctantly, she pulled away from him and moved away. "But for now, I've got to run. I should be back by one or so…"

"I'll be waiting," he said as his body tightened painfully, throbbing and aching with each hard slam of his heartbeat.

"Great. Good." Nodding, she backed away from him and Connor's gaze swept down, loving the look of her long, toned legs in those very tiny shorts.

She made it to the doorway and paused. Turning back to him, she gave him a warning stare. "No more sampling the goodies."

"You're the only goodie I'm interested in," he said quietly.

"Oh, boy." She swallowed hard, then left the room at a run, as if she didn't trust herself to stay another minute.

Nine

By the time she got back to the mansion on the cliff, Dina was exhausted and triumphant. She'd picked up two more jobs just on the strength of her appetizers. It really was amazing what you could get done when you had a little help. With Louise watching the triplets all day, Dina had been able to get everything done in half the time it usually took her when she also had to care for the babies.

She let herself in and paused long enough to listen to the silence in the big house. Then she took the stairs in the darkness; the only lights burning were night-lights plugged into wall sockets and gleaming like fallen stars in the shadows. Dina looked at Connor's door, then at her own, and hesitated.

In that moment, his door opened and a slice of light spilled out. He leaned one hand high on the doorjamb and cocked his head as he looked at her. "You weren't going to back out, were you?"

"I was thinking about it," she admitted, giving a quick glance at the triplets' room, its door cracked open just a bit.

"I've got the monitor in here, so," Connor said, with a sly smile, "if you want to be able to hear them tonight, you'll have to be with me."

Dina had thought about nothing but this moment on the long drive back. There hadn't been much traffic and so she'd let her mind wander a little. Of course, it wandered right to Connor and the situation she found herself in.

Ireland had altered everything between them. She'd allowed her relationship with Connor to fundamentally change. She'd slept with him, realized she was in love with him, and still she had no answers to how they would solve the issue of the triplets' custody. She knew he wanted the babies and so did she. Neither of them was willing to give an inch about that, so sleeping together had only confused an already chaotic situation.

But she couldn't regret it, either. Couldn't wish that she'd stayed away from him. These last two days, sleeping alone in her own room had been difficult. She'd wanted to be with him but hadn't wanted to assume that he meant to keep their intimate relationship alive.

Now she knew he did want what she did and it changed…nothing. There were still too many questions. Too many possible pitfalls to count.

"So," he asked, pushing away from the doorjamb and standing straight. The light from the bedroom behind him made the edges of his silhouette gleam brightly. "I can see you thinking from here. Hell, I can almost hear your thoughts crashing through your mind."

Good thing he couldn't tell *what* she was thinking, Dina told herself.

"There's a lot to consider," she said.

"Not really." He walked toward her, taking long, slow steps. His bare feet made no sound on the carpeted hall floor. When he reached her side, he laid his hands on her shoulders and the heat of him slid through her system, chasing away all of her doubts. Questions. At least for the moment.

"We already crossed this bridge, Dina," he said softly, gaze locked with hers. "It would be crazy to try to go backward now and pretend it didn't happen."

"Or was it crazy to cross the bridge in the first place?"

One corner of his mouth tipped up. "Too late to wonder about that, too. Come with me, Dina," he said. "Be with me."

There never had been a real choice for her, she acknowledged silently. It didn't seem to matter that this could all blow up in her face. For now, she could have what she wanted and needed. She could have Connor. However this ended between them, what she could have *now* was too tempting to ignore.

"Yes," she said and walked beside him to his room.

A couple of hours later, she lay curled up against him, listening to the thundering beat of his heart beneath her ear. Her body was still trembling, her blood still buzzing with the force of the release she'd found only moments earlier.

The night was quiet but for the soft, snuffling sounds coming from the baby monitor on Connor's dresser.

Moonlight streamed through the windows as a soft breeze carried the scent of the ocean.

Her gaze swept what she could see of his room from her position. The bed was as big as a lake, and there was a bay window, with a cushioned window seat, inviting a person to curl up, relax and enjoy the view of the ocean and the beach below. There were tables, chairs, a black marble fireplace against one wall and a door she supposed led to a private bath. It was plush, luxurious and comfy all at once.

And yet, she couldn't relax. Now that her body was replete, her mind was busy, racing with thoughts that jumbled together as if they'd been thrown into the air and allowed to drop into a heap.

"You're thinking again."

"Guilty," she murmured on a soft laugh.

"Well," Connor whispered, "I've been thinking, too."

She tipped her head back on his chest to look up at him and met his gaze warily. "About?"

"This. Us. Where we are and what we want."

"That's a lot of thoughts," she said and didn't know whether to be relieved or concerned that he was spending time worrying over the same things she was.

"Things between us are different now than they were in the beginning," he said.

"That's fair." It was a giant understatement, like saying the ocean was big and wet, but okay. She waited, wondering where he was going with this.

He went up on one elbow and looked down at her. He dropped his left arm across her middle as if trying to keep her at her side, even though she had no intention of moving.

"The custody issue is still staring at us."

"Yeah…" Wary now, every cell in her body went on red alert, prepared for anything.

"We should get married."

"What?" Okay, not prepared for *everything*. For one brief, shining moment, she thought—was he in love with her, too? Was this some magical happy ending to a fairy tale she hadn't even realized she was living? For that moment, her heart lifted, worries sailed away and in seconds, fantasies spun in her head like crystallized sugar—and then shattered just as easily.

"It's the only logical solution."

Logic. She actually heard her fantasies pop like soap bubbles.

"In what universe?" Why were they having this conversation *naked*?

Dina scooted up into a sitting position, drawing the edge of his midnight-blue duvet with her, holding it up to cover herself. She'd gone from blissful to dreamy to completely lost in about ten seconds flat.

He grinned and her heart jolted. This would be so much easier on her if she just didn't love him.

"We both want the kids," he said. "We want each other. This could work."

She couldn't believe he was even suggesting it. Married? They couldn't get married.

"Before you say no," he said as if he could read her mind, "think about this. We each get something out of this marriage."

"This is crazy."

He shook his head. "Not crazy. Brilliant."

She choked back a laugh. Honestly, she still didn't know what to say to him. A simple *no* didn't seem wise. He was still in a position of power when it came to the triplets. It all came down to a custody suit and Dina knew there wasn't a judge in California who would choose her—a woman with a failing business and too many bills—over a rich father willing to do anything to keep the babies. Yet at the same time, how could she say yes?

"This way, I get total access to my kids."

"And I get…?"

"You get the kids, too, and the help you need when you need it," he said. "Look at how much cooking you did yesterday. With Louise to watch the babies, you were able to work without interruption."

"True," she acknowledged, "but that's hardly a reason to get *married*."

"But there's more," he continued. "My house has more than enough room for all of us. You and the triplets would have outgrown that tiny cottage in six months."

"Yes, but—"

He kept talking, plowing right over her as if she hadn't said a word. "You and I wouldn't have to go to war over them."

"True, but—"

"And," he added with a wicked grin that sent shards of light glinting in his eyes, "you have to admit, the sex is great."

"Sure, but—"

"Then there's your dream of opening a restaurant. I can help with that. I'll back you."

Something cold settled in the middle of her chest. Suspicion trickled through her bloodstream. "Why would you do that?"

He shrugged. "Hey, I had that soup you made for dinner. Incredible. Tasted that burrito—were there any of those left over, by the way?"

"No." One word, forced through gritted teeth. She didn't know where he was going with this, but she didn't have a good feeling.

"Too bad." He shifted position on the bed so that he was sitting opposite her. Unlike Dina, who continued to clutch the duvet to hide her nudity from a man who already knew every inch of her body, Connor had no qualms about having this conversation naked.

She told herself not to let her gaze drop below his neck. She was going to need focus and concentration to keep on top of this little chat. And being distracted by his muscled, tanned body wasn't going to help her with that.

"Anyway, to answer your question, I'm willing to back you in a restaurant because you're a talented chef."

"Uh-huh." Her breath was coming fast and shallow.

"Then you won't have to worry about the catering business failing. You can just end it."

"Is that right?" Suddenly, that sexual heat they shared wasn't as much of an issue. God, she was an idiot. She was feeling all warm and fuzzy and he was thinking strategies. "I can quit. Let you buy me a restaurant."

"Yeah." He looked so pleased with himself, she wanted to shake him.

Instead, she got a grip on her rising temper and sense of outrage and ground out, "So rather than letting you pay me for the babies, I let you pay me to marry you."

A couple of seconds passed before he said, "What?"

"Unbelievable." She slid off the bed and tugged on the duvet until he lifted himself off it so she could wrap the damn thing around her like a puffy toga. "I told you I wouldn't sell my *family*. What makes you think I would sell *myself*?"

"Whoa, whoa," he said, holding up both hands in a

placating gesture. "Who said anything about you sell-ing yourself?"

"You did. Just now. 'The sex is great. Marry me and I'll buy you a restaurant.'" She pushed her tangled hair back from her face with an impatient gesture. "Seemed pretty clear to me. All I have to do is have sex with you and I get to keep the kids I love and, oh, boy, have my dreams fulfilled."

"That's insulting."

"You're right about that."

"To *both* of us," he clarified. Shaking his head, he jumped off his side of the bed and came around the end of it to stop right in front of her. "It amazes me. Why is it that people with no money are so damned defensive?"

She gasped. "Seriously? You think the problem here is *me*? Why is it that people with too *much* money are so damned arrogant?"

"I'm not being arrogant, I'm being helpful," he argued.

"Not what it sounds like on *this* side of the check-book."

"You're taking this all wrong."

"Must be because I'm so defensive," she muttered and kicked the duvet away from her feet so she could pace. She couldn't stand still another minute. Her in-sides were jumping, her blood felt as if it were boiling and Dina could have sworn that the edges of her vision really were red.

"Not exactly the response I was expecting from a proposal."

"Not exactly the kind of proposal every girl dreams of hearing."

"Hold on here," he said. "I'm not talking about love. I'm talking about a business deal, via marriage."

She stopped at the bay window and whipped her head around to shoot him a glare that should have frozen him on the spot. "Oh, you've made that perfectly clear."

"Why the hell are you acting like this?"

"Amazing that you can't figure it out."

He huffed out a breath and set both hands at his naked hips. "I'm not trying to buy you, Dina."

"Really? Then why do you keep throwing your money at me?"

"What am I supposed to do," he demanded, tossing his hands high, "pretend I don't have any?"

"You'd never be able to pull it off anyway," she grumbled. Dina stared out the window at the night. Stars studded the sky and the moonlit ocean frothed and churned like the emotions inside her.

"You know, this backward snob thing is getting old."

"Excuse me?" She turned around to look at him through narrowed eyes.

He laughed a little, but the sound held no humor. "You know just what I'm saying. You're threatened by my bank account."

That was true. With money came power, and no one knew that better than those who didn't have any. "Well, who wouldn't be?"

"I'm offering to marry you, share the kids with you and help you make your restaurant dream come true." He shook his head. "How does that make me the bad guy?"

"Not bad…" she said, "just dictatorial, and overbearing." Dina's hair was really bugging her. She stabbed her fingers through the heavy mass and pushed it back and away from her face. "I don't need you to tell me when to end my business or to buy me a restaurant. I can make my own dreams come true."

"And I can help. What's wrong with that?"

"Because you want me to do something because you think it's the right thing to do and I should just fall in line."

"Where the hell did that come from?" he demanded.

Dina knew where it came from. Years of watching her mother change her life, her hair, her personality, her laugh, all to please the man she was with at the time. She did it for so long, the woman she was at the heart of her had faded and blurred like a photo left in the sun. Finally, it was as if she'd disappeared completely, dissolving into one of the faux women she'd pretended to be.

Dina wouldn't do that. Wouldn't allow her attraction to Connor to morph into the identity-crushing thing her mother had lived through.

"You don't have to open a damn restaurant," he argued. "Keep the catering business..."

"Thanks so much." She folded her arms under her breasts and tapped the toes of one bare foot against the rug. "Are you sure a *caterer* is good enough to marry one of the Kings of California?"

"Good enough?"

"Can't have one of you married to some lowly caterer, can we?"

"You're nuts. I've got a cousin married to the cookie queen, another one's wife owns a Christmas tree farm and I could go on, but what's the point? This isn't about *me*. This is about you and whatever the hell's going on inside your head." Shaking his head he added, "Hell, make tacos and sell 'em at a stand in front of the house. I don't care."

"Wow, thank you again." Dina didn't believe him. He was maneuvering her until she was in just the spot he wanted her to be. Her heart hurt and yet in spite of this awful argument, she still loved him. She probably always would. Which was just so depressing.

"So I'm damned if I want to help and damned if I don't?"

She clutched the duvet even more tightly to her, fisting one hand in the silky fabric. Making sure her voice was steady, she took a breath and said, "You want too much."

"I want my family," he corrected, "and I'm willing to include you in that. What's the problem?"

She couldn't tell him that. Couldn't tell him that she loved him, because he didn't want to hear it. Couldn't say that a business proposal broke her heart even while it tempted her to accept. Because he wanted too much and didn't give enough.

"Connor, you can't marry someone just to solve a custody dispute."

"Why the hell not?" He waved one hand at the rumpled bed behind him. "Tell me that what we have together is not the best sex of your life."

She couldn't. Frowning at the bed, she tried not to think about what they'd been doing there so amazingly just a little while ago. "Sex isn't a reason for people to be together, either."

"Sure it is. And a damn good one." He blew out a breath, folded his arms across his chest and braced his bare feet wide apart.

She was still deliberately not looking at his body.

"Dina, you're reacting emotionally."

"Well, yeah."

"If you look at it rationally instead, you'll see this makes perfect sense. We get along fine. This house is

perfect for kids and will be even better after my cousin
Rafe builds out a triplet suite—"

She rolled her eyes. There went his checkbook again,
waving back and forth in front of her face.

"—we have great sex. I like you. You like me."

Not right now, she didn't. Love, yes. Like? Not so
much.

Outside the windows, surf pounded against the rocks
at the base of the cliffs and sounded like the universe
sighing. He kept talking and his voice, low and persua-
sive, meshed with the sighs of the sea.

"We'll never have to fight over the kids, Dina," he
said in a near-seductive tone. "We can share them. Share
everything."

Her gaze flicked up to his. Ice-blue eyes stared at her
and she felt herself falling into those alluring depths. She
loved him. She couldn't tell him that because he wouldn't
want to hear it and she didn't want to give him that much
power over her anyway. But was one-sided love enough
to make a marriage any damn good? Even a marriage
of convenience?

"Think about it," he said, skimming the fingers of his
right hand along her cheek before pulling her up against
his body and holding her there. He held her head to his
chest, and she heard his heartbeat again. Steady, regular,
calm. "Just think about it, okay?"

That was the problem. Dina was pretty sure she
wouldn't be able to think of anything else.

"Say yes." The very next morning, Angelica Cortez
smiled at her granddaughter from across the table at a
local coffee bar. "Why wouldn't you say yes?"

"Because he doesn't love me," Dina answered, stirring cream into her coffee and watching the clouds of white dissolve into the darkness.

"But you love him."

Her head jerked up and her gaze fixed on her grandmother. "I never said that."

"I'm not blind, *nieta*," the older woman said softly.

The coffee bar was crowded, mostly with people coming or going from the beach. In late June it was still cool, but not cold enough to keep the surfers at bay. There was a thin coating of gritty sand on the floor and every time someone opened the front door, a brisk wind entered, reminding everyone that it wasn't the heart of summer yet.

Dina had slipped out of the house early, thanking heaven that Louise was willing and eager to spend time with the triplets. Dina needed some time with her grandmother, the most rational human being on the planet, and she knew she wouldn't get much talking done if she had to chase the babies around.

Connor was meeting his cousin Rafe at the house to start the renovations. And things seemed to be rolling along whether or not Dina was ready to accept them. Once he had the triplets' suite completed, he would go for full custody—she knew it. The only way to forestall that was to marry him. But how could she do that knowing the marriage would never be what she might want it to be?

Now, looking into her grandmother's understanding eyes, Dina sighed. "Fine. I love him. But isn't that one more reason to *not* marry him?"

Her grandmother laughed, clearly amused. "Love is the only reason to marry," the older woman told her with a shake of her head. "You and he, you love the children. You are living together now anyway..."

Amazing that having her grandmother know that she was sleeping with someone could make Dina blush, but there it was.

"Why not be married?"

"Because it would be a contract," Dina said, taking a sip of her coffee. "A business agreement."

"An arranged marriage," Angelica said, nodding. "Your grandfather and I, ours was an arranged marriage also. That worked out well for both of us for forty-seven years."

Dina sighed. "Abuela, that's different."

"How? You already love him, *nieta*. This is not a bad thing."

"It could be."

"And it could be wonderful. You won't know until you try."

"And if we try and fail, the babies suffer."

"Then don't fail." Angelica reached across the table and took Dina's hand in hers. "Many arranged marriages become unions of love. Why shouldn't yours?"

Because Connor didn't want a wife. He wanted a bed partner. A co-parent. And because even loving him, there was a part of Dina waiting for Connor to turn on her. To insist she be other than what she was.

"You're not your mother," Angelica said quietly, and still her voice carried over the clash and clang of coffee cups, the espresso machine and the muted conversations going on all around them. "Trust him. Better still, trust yourself."

Two weeks later, Dina's new last name was King.

The wedding was small, only family and a few friends. Connor's backyard was transformed with white ribbon, summer flowers and tables and chairs clustered across the wide, manicured expanse of lawn. The sun was out, music soared from outdoor speakers and their guests were helping themselves to the buffet table that Dina had prepared.

"Your new wife is a hell of a cook."

Connor glanced at Colt, then shifted his gaze back to where Dina, in a long strapless cream-colored dress, danced with Sage clutched tightly to her. The other two kids were being passed around the family while his cousins' kids raced through the crowd, laughing.

"She really is," Connor said, not taking his gaze off of Dina. Her dress clung lovingly to the lush curves he couldn't wait to get his hands on again. Her long dark brown hair flowed and swayed around her shoulders as she danced with the tiny boy in her arms. When she tipped her head back to laugh, the line of her throat was an elegant column that made him want to lick the length of it.

His body went tight and hard and he was forced to tear his gaze from her before it became impossible to hide his reaction to her.

"Couldn't talk her into hiring a caterer," Connor told his twin. "She insisted on doing it all herself."

"And I for one, am grateful." Colton picked up another miniburrito and popped it into his mouth. Grinning around it, he said, "She's also gorgeous."

"Yeah, she is."

"Never thought I'd see you get married, though."

"It's business, Colt," Connor told him, looking back at Dina because he just couldn't help himself. "I explained it to you."

"Right. Business." Colt elbowed his twin. "That's why you're drooling."

"I'm not—" Connor broke off, took a sip of a cold beer and then said, "I never wanted to get married because I'd never be able to trust a woman enough. But if this is business, then I risk nothing." He shrugged, looked at Dina as she handed Sage off to Louise and swung Sam into the dance. Tenderness ached in his heart, but he ignored it and said, "If Dina screws up, I'll divorce her and keep the kids. If everything goes right, we have great sex with no messy emotions. It's a win-win."

The idea of divorcing his brand-new bride gave Con a cold feeling in the center of his gut, but he ignored it. He still wasn't sure what had finally convinced Dina to marry him, but he suspected he had Angelica Cortez to thank for that. And now that they were married, he'd make sure divorce didn't come into the picture. He watched Dina and felt the cold ease away into heat that seemed to be with him all the damn time now. It wasn't just desire, it was more. It went deeper than want, richer than like, but trying to pin a name to what he was feeling only made him more uncomfortable, so he let that go, too.

Colt just stared at him for a long minute, then shook his head and scooped up a tortilla chip loaded with seven-layer dip. Taking a bite, he said, "You're an idiot. Marriage is about more than sex, Connor. It's about talking together, laughing together and *trust*. You're already talking about divorce."

"No, I'm not," he argued, though a slight ping of guilt jabbed at him. "I'm just saying, I can't lose here."

"Sure you can." Colt finished off the last of his food,

shrugged and said, "But you'll figure it out. I have faith. Right now, though, I'm going to go dance with my wife. Maybe you should think about doing the same."

Ten

Dina's life changed almost instantly.

Being married to a King opened doors that she hadn't even known about. Suddenly, her catering business was busier than ever. She wanted to be annoyed that it was the King name, not her own cooking abilities that were getting attention. But she was too happy with the results.

Catering her own wedding hadn't been easy, but how could she call herself a caterer and then hire someone else for her big day? So she'd worked for two days and with Louise's help had pulled it off. Not only had everyone at the wedding loved the food, but two of the guests had called a few days later to hire her for their own parties.

But as much as her business was already looking healthier after a month of marriage, she was still on edge, worried about whether or not she'd done the right thing. Loving Connor was a part of her now. Something that had worked its way into every cell of her body, and there was no denying or ignoring it. But being in love didn't make her blind, either.

Connor wasn't interested in love. He'd made that plain enough. And since the wedding, she'd sometimes caught him looking at her in such a thoughtful way that she wondered what the heck he was thinking. But he remained the same man he was before. Irritating. Charming. Seductive. And when he took her to bed every night in the room they shared, he managed to banish the doubts that nibbled at her during the day.

Sitting on a quilt spread under a tree in the backyard, she watched as the trips ran in circles, laughing and babbling at each other. The three babies were happy and healthy and they loved Connor and their new home. The five of them were meshing into a unit and while she loved it, Dina worried about what would happen if it all fell apart. Still, it was moments like these when she told herself that marrying Connor had been a good decision.

From the house came thundering crashes, the high-pitched whine of saws and shouts from the crew of workmen. King Construction was busily tearing out walls and expanding the triplets' bedroom into what would be a suite that would grow with them. The noise was deafening, but they were working at top speed and would probably be finished in another couple of weeks.

Everything in Dina's world had changed.

And while it was exciting, it also made her feel vulnerable.

Maybe it hadn't been the brightest move, to marry knowing her husband didn't love her, but she couldn't regret it. She had the triplets. She had Connor. And she had a business that was booming. She'd be crazy to complain.

Surrounded by sippy cups, cookies and bowls of sliced bananas, Dina picked up her legal-size pad of paper and her favorite pen. She loved her laptop and her tablet, but when she really wanted to feel creative and let her mind flow, she needed pen and paper.

Idly, she started sketching out menu ideas for the start-of-summer open house party at a local realty office. Glancing from the pad to the kids, she smiled as she began listing ingredients she'd need.

When she heard the heart-wrenching scream, Dina dropped everything and ran.

Connor had a stack of files to go through and sign and a lunch meeting in less than a half hour. Once that meeting was over, though, he was thinking about blowing off the rest of the day and skipping out early. He smiled at the thought, since he was always the responsible one around here. Come in early, stay late, build the business. He hadn't really had a *life* until the triplets and Dina had shaken up his world. And now that he had them, he resented being away from them.

Two days ago, they'd all gone down to the beach and Connor smiled to himself, remembering. The triplets had loved the sand, the water, the seagulls. He could still hear Sadie giggling as he held her toes into the frigid ocean. Sage had been more interested in eating the sand, but Sam had loved knocking down every castle Connor and Dina had built for them.

His smile softened, deepened as he remembered Dina in her oh so tiny electric blue bikini. Oh yeah, maybe he'd leave early and they could all make another trip to the beach.

He'd never even considered getting married in the

past, but so far, it wasn't bad. Except, of course, for the growing feeling that he was becoming more and more deeply attached to his wife. Just the thought of her made him smile, and wasn't that another worry? He'd never had a woman in his life that he not only liked but couldn't wait to see. He'd never before felt that quick rush of excitement when she walked into a room.

It was a little unnerving to admit, even to himself, just how much her presence in his life affected him.

"Con."

He looked up to see Colt, grim faced and steely eyed, standing in the open doorway of his office. Instantly, fear slithered down Connor's spine like drops of ice water rolling along his skin. Pushing up out of his chair, he demanded, "What's wrong?"

"Louise called." Colt winced as he added, "Sam got hurt and Dina took him to the emergency room."

Cold grabbed Connor and filled him, head to toe. He felt bathed in icy water and struggled to draw a breath. Fear. So rich, so raw, it closed his throat. An image of the tiny boy filled his mind. So easygoing. So happy. So dangerously vulnerable. Con forced his legs to work, walking around his desk, headed for the door. "How bad is he hurt? What the hell happened? Why didn't Dina call me?"

"She tried—" Colt followed him as Con walked through the front office. "You were on the phone with a client and Linda didn't put her through."

"I'm so sorry," their admin said from her desk, tears pooling in her eyes. "She didn't tell me—"

"It's okay." Con didn't have time to soothe Linda. He looked at his twin. "I'm headed to the hospital."

"I know." Colt slapped his shoulder. "Call me when you know something."

"Right." He was out the door and across the parking lot in seconds. Less than a minute later, he was on Pacific Coast Highway headed south. Thankfully, their office was in Laguna Beach, only a few short miles from the local hospital. Every one of those miles felt like a hundred to Con.

His mind filled with images designed to torture him. Sam bleeding. Dina sobbing, all alone in a sterile room, hovering over the baby boy they both loved so much. In his mind, Con heard Sam screaming and the sympathetic wails from his brother and sister.

Con's heart jackhammered in his chest and his fists flexed convulsively on the wheel as he tore in and out of traffic, ignoring yellow lights, punching the accelerator when he had a chance for more speed. Fear snapped at the edges of his heart.

He whipped into the parking lot, parked outside the emergency room and didn't give a damn if they towed his car. He had to get to Dina. To Sam. He hit the automatic double doors at a run, sprinted to the reception desk with a quick look in the waiting area. No Dina. No Sam. Just kids and adults, crying, worried. He knew how they felt. He slammed both hands on the desk and barked, "Sam King. Cortez. Where is he?"

The older woman took one look at him and her eyebrows lifted. "Which is it? Cortez or King?"

He took a breath, summoned a semblance of calm and said, "Cortez. Soon to be King. And why does this matter? He's a baby. He's hurt. I'm his father."

For a second or two it looked as though she might argue with him, but she must have seen the desperation in his eyes and taken pity. Whatever worked, Con thought wildly. Hell, if he'd had to, he'd have offered to build a wing to the damn place if it meant they'd get him to Sam.

"Exam room two. On the left."

He spun away from the desk, ignored the stench of misery and antiseptic and headed for the designated room. He burst inside and Dina whirled around to face him, Sam clutched in her arms. The baby's face was red and streaked with tears, his breath hitching in and out of his little chest. His black hair stood up on end and the moment he saw Connor, he reached out both chubby arms. "Da!"

Con's already unsteady heart lurched, but he snatched the little boy from Dina and cuddled him close. *Da*. Sam had just said his first word and the magic of that briefly swamped the building fear. For one moment Con inhaled the soft, clean scent of Sam and let his own heart drop to a more normal rhythm as he felt the little boy's warm, solid weight. Sam laid his head on Con's shoulder with a breathy sigh and Con looked to Dina.

"What happened?"

Tears had left their mark behind on her face as well. Her big brown eyes were still wet with them. Her bottom lip trembled. "They were playing in the backyard. I was right there, Con. Everything was fine, then Sam screamed and when I went to pick him up, his leg was bleeding and—"

Connor shifted his grip on the baby and for the first time noticed a hastily wrapped, bloodstained bandage. Sam sniffled and Connor patted his back gently, hoping to soothe.

Shaking his head, Connor asked, "How did it happen? What cut him? Did you see it?"

She nodded. "A nail in the grass. A big one, like a roofing nail," she said. "It must have come from the construction on the house." Shaking her head furiously, she said, "I should have thought of that. Been more careful. Realized that this was a possibility."

She was beating herself up so badly, Connor's heart hurt for her. Without even thinking about it, he snaked his free arm out and drew her into his chest, holding her tight alongside Sam. "Not your fault. I didn't think of it, either. But I'm going to talk to Rafe. Tell him I want one of his guys running a damn metal detector across the grass every night when they're done for the day."

She shook her head against him. "They're not going to want to do that."

"I'll pay extra."

She laughed a little and looked up at him. "Okay, sometimes your checkbook comes in handy."

He smiled and kissed the top of her head. "Accidents happen." With the two of them held tightly to him, Connor said, "Remind me sometime to tell you about all the times Colt and I ended up in the emergency ward. Our mom used to say they were going to give us our own rooms."

He felt her relax a little and smiled in spite of everything. Sam was hurt, but he wasn't in danger. He would heal. And Dina was here in Connor's arms, and for the first time since his brother had walked into the office with grim eyes, Con took an easy breath.

"So what's the doctor say?" he asked.

"Nothing." She tipped her head back to look at him. "We haven't seen anyone yet."

"That's unacceptable," he said. "You take Sam. I'll find a doctor and get him in here—"

The door opened and a young woman with a warm smile, copper-colored hair and a teddy bear on her stethoscope walked in. "Hi, I'm Dr. Lamb." She checked the chart in her hands, then looked at the baby. "This must be Sam."

The little boy lifted his head, glanced at her, then buried his face in Connor's shoulder again.

Every protective instinct he possessed rose to the surface. Sam expected Con to take care of him, keep him safe. Hating to let go of the boy at all, especially when tiny hands fisted in his shirt and hung on, Con had to force himself to sit Sam down on the examining table.

Dr. Lamb dug into a nearby drawer and pulled out a tiny stuffed animal still in protective plastic wrap. She freed the elephant, then bent down to look Sam in the eye as she handed it to him. "Why don't you hold onto this while I look at your leg, okay?"

Warily, Sam took the stuffed animal and held it tightly in both hands. Connor gave Dina's hand a squeeze, then reluctantly released her so they could each take up a post on either side of the young doctor. Connor felt helpless and he hated it. He couldn't *do* anything and that tore at him. He scrubbed one hand across the back of his neck and watched the doctor examine Sam with gentle fingers.

When she was finished, she said, "Well, looks like we're going to need a few stitches."

"Oh, no," Dina whispered.

"No worries," the doctor said, smiling for Sam's benefit. "We've got a numbing spray. He won't feel a thing, I promise. Are his immunizations up-to-date?"

Connor blanked. "I have no idea." He turned to Dina.

"Yes," she said. "He's had the usual shots and vaccines. I didn't bring his records with me, but if I can use your computer, I can get them for you."

"That's all right. I think we'll give him a small-dose tetanus booster, just to be on the safe side."

While the doctor got busy and Dina kept Sam distracted, Connor watched and realized that if Dina hadn't been there, he wouldn't have had a clue about Sam's medical history. There was still so much he had to learn. Discover. And he had to arrange to legally adopt his kids, make sure they carried his name.

He looked at Dina as she comforted Sam and played with the stuffed elephant. She was a wonderful mother to the triplets and she was a hell of a woman. And they were married now, so she should probably adopt the three of them, too. Make it official. All of them Kings. A family.

He was grateful Dina was here with him, sharing the worry, the anxiety. He'd always been the kind of man to stand on his own. To take care of business and to never allow panic to creep in and get a grip on him. But he'd never had kids before, either, and now that he did, Connor knew that fear would always be his closest companion. Having Dina there eased something in him that he hadn't even known existed, though. She had, in the short time he'd known her, dug deeper inside Connor than anyone else ever had.

Just then, as if she'd sensed him watching her, Dina looked over at him and smiled, and in response, Connor's heart did a hard, irrevocable tumble. She quickly turned her attention back to Sam, but the damage had been done. That smile of hers, those open, beautiful dark eyes, the easy warmth that surrounded her had finally pushed past Connor's last line of defense.

And it was there, in that small, crowded room rich

with the scent of antiseptic, that he realized he couldn't ignore the terrifying truth any longer.

He was a man in love with his wife.

A fact that shook him to his bones.

All right. Since that moment in the emergency room two weeks before, Connor had been able to admit—at least to himself—that he loved Dina. He could accept that. But he still didn't trust her, so he kept his feelings to himself. He kept waiting for her to make a mistake. To prove to him that she was just like every other female he'd known in his life.

Yet so far…she hadn't.

Instead, she continued to show him that she was just who she claimed to be. Strong. Independent. Loving. So why couldn't he relax his guard?

He couldn't love her without being at risk—and as long as she didn't know how he felt, that risk was mitigated. *Cowardly?* his mind whispered. *No. Smart*, he argued sternly. He'd been used too many times to let down his defenses, even if Dina was like no one else. She wasn't interested in his money. Had been insulted any time he'd tried to help her financially.

But how did he know if that was for real? Maybe it was a well-performed act and she was just lulling him into complacency. Okay, that sounded stupid even to him. But he still couldn't bring himself to trust her completely. How could he be expected to? He hadn't even known her until a little more than a month ago. So he'd bide his time. Give it a few months. Maybe a year. If she really was who she claimed to be, then he'd tell her he loved her. He just needed to be sure.

He'd had Dina cater the party for fifty of his most

important business associates and he'd had nothing but compliments all night—not just on the food but on his good fortune in marrying her. Between Dina and the event planner she'd worked with, the party had been a huge success.

Most of the guests were gone now, and as two men left, Connor overheard their low-pitched conversation.

"Yeah, who knew Connor King would ever get married?"

"And to a woman with kids," his friend said. "You really think they're his?"

"Who knows?" the first man said, and Connor stepped deeper into the shadows so he could listen without being seen. "I'll tell you what, though, if I could get a woman like that in my bed, I'd take her even if she was lying to my face. Wouldn't be the first time a woman with nothing married a man with money just to make life easier."

The second guy said, "If you're gonna get used, get used by a woman who can cook like *this* and looks like she does."

They were gone a moment later and Connor stepped out to say goodbye to the rest of his guests. But that conversation kept echoing in his mind. People were talking. He'd expected that. They were saying he was being used. Was he?

"It was a wonderful party, Connor. Thanks for having us."

"My pleasure," he said, shaking hands with David Halliwell, one of his clients.

The August night was warm, but the ocean breeze kept it comfortable. There were white fairy lights strung through the trees and strings and piano music still soaring from the speakers. Guests were beginning to leave and frankly, he was ready to be alone with his wife. Maybe he was wrong. Maybe it was time he told her that he loved her. Take that risk.

"Your wife is a genius," Marian Halliwell was saying. "In fact, I've hired her to do our anniversary party next month and my sister is going to call her in for the grand opening of her boutique in September."

He felt a swift flash of pride. "I'm sure she's looking forward to it."

"Oh, she is," Marian practically cooed. "I told her now that she's a King, the world is going to open up for her."

"Is that right?" He flicked a glance across the yard to where Dina was supervising the cleanup.

"Well, she already knew that, of course," Marian continued. "She said herself that becoming a King was the best business decision she'd ever made."

He looked back at the middle-aged woman. "Did she?" A slender thread of suspicion began to uncoil inside Connor. *Business decision.* She'd married him, gotten his name, and now was building her business into the kind of success she'd only dreamed about before. He had offered her a straight business deal proposal and she'd turned that down, insulted. Now it seemed she was okay with the business aspect and he was the one who wanted this marriage to be about more.

"Come on, Marian," her husband said, steering her toward the door. "Time to go."

"Of course," his wife agreed, looking back over her shoulder as she walked away. "Tell Dina I'll be calling her to go over details."

He nodded and waved, but wasn't really paying attention anymore. Doubts assailed him, and though he didn't want to admit to it, Connor realized that Marian's throwaway comment had shaken him. His go-to emotion of cautious mistrust rose to the surface and neatly displaced the whole notion of telling Dina about how he felt.

Across the yard, she moved through the moonlight, the tiny, flickering white lights above her, and she looked like a dream. The kind of dream a man might convince himself to believe in even if it wasn't real.

As he watched, a man approached her and steered her toward the shadows. Instinct drove Connor across the yard, ignoring the two or three caterer's helpers stacking chairs and carrying dishes into the kitchen. His gaze fixed solely on the bushes and the man trying to tug Dina farther into them, Connor hurried forward. But what would he find? Was Dina in on this little rendezvous?

"Nice party."

Dina cringed, but forced a brittle smile as she turned to face the man who'd spoken. For the last half hour, everywhere she went, there he was. He was about forty, wearing a suit that probably cost more than the rent on her old bungalow. He also, thanks to too many trips to the margarita bar, seemed to think he was irresistible.

"Thanks," she said, "I'm glad you're having a good time."

"Connor always did have all the luck with women," the man said, moving in closer and reaching out to stroke her arm.

Dina stepped back, but he moved with her and she realized that they were alone in this shadow-filled corner of the yard. "Thanks, but if you'll excuse me—"

"You don't have to run away," the man said, reaching out to take her arm in a firm grip. "I've got as much money as ol' Connor. You and me could have some fun."

"Excuse me?" She tried to yank her arm free, but he was strong in spite of being drunk. This was a fine line to walk, she thought. She didn't want to cause a scene, but she also didn't like being manhandled.

"Come on, just give me a little kiss and I'll leave you alone."

"You can leave me alone without the kiss," she told him. Honestly, she just wanted him gone and this night over. It was an important party for Connor's clients and she didn't want to ruin it by creating a scene. But if this man didn't let her go, she was going to start kicking and screaming.

"One kiss. What's the big deal?"

"Get off of me," she said, trying to pull free.

"But you're so pretty," he was saying and maneuvered her around until his back was to the party and hiding her from sight. "One kiss. You'll like it."

"No, I—" He bent his head and Dina jerked back, but before the man's mouth met hers, he was yanked away and tossed to one side.

She looked up into Connor's furious features and her heart swelled. Feminism be damned, there was something to be said for having a white knight of your very own ride to your rescue. It was over quickly, with the drunk already scrambling to his feet, mumbling apologies and escaping. Thank heaven that most of the guests had already left. She glanced around the yard and realized that she and Connor were alone. Most of the cleanup was finished and the crew would leave right after.

"Thank you," she said, shifting her gaze back to Connor's. "He was just drunk, but—"

Then she noticed the harsh light in Connor's eyes and

the grim slash of his mouth. He was still furious. But not at the guy he'd already vanquished…at *her*.

"Connor?"

His features went even colder. "We'll talk about this later. When everyone's gone. Meet me in the great room."

She watched him stalk across the yard, never once looking back at her. A yawning emptiness opened up inside her and still, she had to breathe. Had to move, had to help finish the cleanup. But she felt as if her feet were encased in cement. She was hurt and confused and working slowly toward the anger that Con obviously had already carefully banked inside him. What the heck was going on?

By the time the servers were gone, it was late. The triplets were upstairs asleep, Louise was tucked up in her own suite and the entire house felt dark and silent. Dina put the last of the dishes into the dishwasher, set it to run and only then did she allow herself to even think again about what had happened earlier.

The hurt was still with her, but her anger was now free to build and quickly outpaced the ache in her heart. She had done nothing wrong, yet he was clearly mad at her. Well, she could match him in that at the moment. In the quiet house, the hum of the dishwasher was overly loud and chased her out of the kitchen. Her steps clicked quietly against the hardwood floor as she walked along the hall to the great room at the front of the house, where Connor had asked her to meet him.

He was standing in front of the wide windows, staring out at the night beyond the glass. His hands were tucked into his slacks and if she hadn't known him well enough to see the tension radiating off him, she might have thought him relaxed.

"Connor?"

Slowly, he swiveled his head to look over his shoulder at her and his expression looked as if it had been carved in stone. His handsome features were tight and hard and there was no welcome in those ice-blue eyes.

"If you're going to cheat on me," he said, keeping his voice a tight, low hiss, "at least be discreet."

"Cheat?" Stunned surprise rocked her back on her heels, but she recovered quickly. "That's what you thought you saw? Are you crazy?" She took a step forward and stopped again. "The man was drunk and annoying me. There was no *cheating* going on. I was trying to get him off me without creating a huge scene. Couldn't you tell that when you made your grand entrance?"

"What I saw was the two of you headed for the shadows."

"He was pulling me into the bushes."

"And I should believe you."

"Why wouldn't you?" She wouldn't have thought she could be more surprised than she had been earlier by his unjustified anger, but she would have been wrong. "I don't cheat, Connor. And I don't lie."

"Right. You just use people to get what you want."

"What are you talking about?"

He walked toward her. Every step was slow and measured, sounding like a heartbeat in the quiet.

"I thought you were different," he said, moving in on her. "You almost had me fooled. But it was all a setup, wasn't it? You get me to marry you—"

A short, sharp laugh shot from her throat. "Get you to marry me?" she repeated, shocked both at what he was saying and at the cold, dispassionate set of his features. "You're the one who talked me into marrying you—"

"Oh, yeah." He nodded. "You worked that well. Tangle me up in my own sheets, make me want you so bad I can't think straight. Move in here and make yourself a part of my life." He scrubbed one hand across the back of his neck. "You were probably the start of all of it. Why wouldn't you be? You made me so nuts it was easy to maneuver me into proposing—"

"Maneuver you?" Fury didn't even cover what she was feeling. Dina could hardly draw a breath, her chest felt so tight. "You arrogant, conceited…"

"You know what the best part was?" Connor asked with a shake of his head. "Every time I tried to help you financially, your insulted act was impressive."

"Act? I wasn't acting. I didn't want your money then and I don't want it now."

"No, you just wanted my name. That was it all along, wasn't it?" He came even closer but Dina didn't back up. She stood her ground, tipping her chin up so that she could look into the eyes she had thought she knew so well. There was nothing familiar there now. Just suspicion and regret and anger.

She could meet fury with fury or she could dig deep and come up with some sort of calm. Try to make sense of this. Hurt tangled with temper and won. The cold went deep into her bones and she thought she might never be warm again. "I don't know what you're talking about."

"You told Marian Halliwell that marrying me was the best business decision you ever made."

Had she? She didn't remember. She'd talked to so many people at the party, they all sort of blended together. But in a way, that was true. Being married to Connor *had* helped her business grow, even though she hadn't taken Connor's offer of an investment. She'd done the work herself. Being a King wouldn't continue getting her jobs if she couldn't pull them off.

"Using the King name's getting you a lot of new clients lately, isn't it?"

"You've gotten me two of them," she pointed out.

He waved that away. "You're using me, Dina."

"You actually believe that, don't you?" She just stared up at him, her own eyes blurred with a sheen of tears that she refused to let fall. Dina was shaken, disheartened but somehow not disappointed.

"Yeah," he said simply. "I do. You know, when I offered to use my name and contacts to give your business a boost, I meant the offer. But I was actually impressed when you said no." He shook his head slowly. "Turns out though, you just wanted to do the boosting yourself. Did you really think I wouldn't find out how you were milking your new last name for business? Did you think I wouldn't care?"

"I wasn't doing that, Connor." Silently she congratulated herself on keeping her voice quiet and even in spite of how she was trembling. Pain shimmered brightly as her heart simply broke.

A part of Dina had been waiting for the fairy tale to shatter. For Connor to let her down and for reality to come crashing in on her. She loved him, but that wasn't enough. He didn't even know her, she thought sadly. If he did, he never would have believed the worst of her so easily. So she couldn't trust him. And love without trust didn't stand a chance.

"I don't cheat, Connor. I don't lie," she repeated. "And I don't use people." Her gaze locked on his, she tamped down the anger churning within and let the pain color her words as she said, "But you can't see that because you're too busy waiting for people to fail you. You actually went out of your way to twist things around to make me look as guilty as you're afraid I am."

"Afraid?" He scoffed at that.

"Yeah. Afraid." She reached up, but instead of slapping him, she cupped his cheek in her palm. "I recognize the signs because I was scared, too, and tonight, it looks like I was right to be. I didn't use you, Connor. I didn't marry you to help my business or for the sake of the triplets—no matter what you originally offered me. See, the only reason I married you was because I loved you."

He blinked and then his eyes narrowed.

She let her hand drop. "And that disbelieving look in your eye is why I never bothered to tell you."

"What do you want me to say?" he ground out.

"Nothing. You've already said too much," she told him. "It's late. I'm tired. I'm going to bed. In my old room."

She took a couple of steps and stopped when he asked, "Did he hurt you?"

Dina looked over her shoulder at him. "Who?"

"John Ballas. The guy who was bothering you." Connor's face was hard and still. "Did he hurt you?"

Shaking her head, Dina said, "He was just being drunk and foolish. If you hadn't shown up, I could have handled him." She paused and said, "But to answer your question…no. He's not the one who hurt me, Connor."

Eleven

Connor spent the night at the office. It wasn't the first time he'd slept on the wide leather couch. But this time was a misery.

All night he'd lain awake, replaying that scene with Dina, and no matter how many different ways he tried to examine it, he still looked like an idiot. Even if he was right—he'd handled it all wrong.

He didn't even know what had set him off. Con only knew that the last couple of weeks he'd been tense. To be honest, he'd been tense ever since that afternoon when he'd realized he loved her. That had thrown him. Hard. Still, he'd been working through it, pretending that everything was fine. Then his guests had started complimenting him on Dina's talents and saying how they were going to be hiring her for upcoming events. He'd watched her, smiling, happy, connecting with people, and a voice in the back of his mind whispered that she was just using his name to promote herself. That she was no different from any of the other women who had tried to use him in the past.

Pushing up off the couch, he stumbled into the front office and made coffee. But while he performed the familiar task, his mind was dredging up images of Dina. The smile on her face when he'd pulled John Ballas off her and the way that smile had died away because of *Connor*. God.

He leaned both hands on the tabletop and listened with half an ear to the hiss and bubble of the coffeemaker. He'd saved his wife from a jerk and then turned on her. "Who does that?"

"Does what?"

Connor didn't bother to muffle the groan as he looked over at Colt, standing in the doorway. No one would ever think them identical today, he thought in disgust. Colt had clearly slept well. He'd shaved and wasn't still wearing the clothes he'd had on the night before. Plus, his life wasn't currently in the toilet.

"What did you do?"

"What didn't I do?" Connor answered, turning back to watch the rich black liquid drip all too slowly into the waiting pot.

"Seriously, Con. I saw you at the party last night. You were wired so tight I half expected you to give off sparks."

"I know."

"So. I repeat. What did you do?"

"Made an ass of myself, apparently," he muttered, not happy about sharing this moment with his twin.

"Yeah, I guessed that, since Penny talked to Dina this morning."

His head snapped up. He looked at his twin and squinted against the morning sunlight streaming in through the front windows. "Is she okay?"

"Is there some reason she wouldn't be?"

Plenty, he thought but didn't say. There were some things he wasn't going to talk about, even with his twin. "Give me a break, will ya?"

"Sure," Colt agreed quickly. "Arm? Leg? Thick head?"

"Don't be funny," Con muttered. "Not in the mood for funny—thank God. Coffee's done." He grabbed the pot, poured a cup and took that first hesitant yet blissful sip. The heat and caffeine didn't help, though. There was still a black hole of misery in the center of his chest. And being completely awake only made him more aware of it.

"What the hell happened?"

"I don't even know," Con said before he could measure his words. Hell, he'd been going over all of this since the night before and he still couldn't have said exactly why he'd snapped. Shaking his head, he took another sip of coffee before asking, "Penny talked to Dina. How is she?"

"Hurt. Confused. Mad."

He wiped his face with his palm and blew out a breath. "Sure she is. Why wouldn't she be?"

"What's the deal, Connor?"

"I don't know." Colt followed when Connor walked back to his office. Dropping back down onto the couch, he braced his elbows on his knees. "Something had been building up in me for days. Maybe weeks. Last night, I don't know. I just…snapped." He looked up at his twin. "I love her."

"News flash," Colt said wryly.

Scowling, Connor said, "Well, it was news to me. And not happy news." He leaned back on the couch and threw one arm across his eyes. "I didn't want to love her. Too risky. Too messy. So, I don't know, maybe I was looking for reasons to *not* care."

"Why?"

"You can ask me that?" Connor's gaze snapped to his twin's and there was heat in it. "How the hell did you react when you found out Penny had been lying to you? That she'd had your children and never bothered to tell you?"

Colt shifted, clearly uncomfortable. "Different situation."

"No, it isn't. I had three kids out there that I never knew about." Connor set his coffee cup on the low table in front of him with a slap and stood up. "Jackie, my *best friend*, lied to me and disappeared out of my life to hide the lie. She *used* me. If Jackie could do it, why not Dina?"

"So you judge everybody based on Jackie?"

"Not just her." Connor started pacing and while he talked, his anger spiked again and he told himself that maybe he hadn't been wrong at all the night before. "How many women have tried to get their hooks in us? For the money? For our name? For what we can do for them? Hell, have you forgotten how fast you ran from Penny? Didn't your original marriage last a whopping twenty-four hours before you bolted?" Connor stabbed his index finger toward his brother. "You told me that you loved Penny even then, but you didn't trust it. Didn't trust *her*. So you ran."

"This isn't about me," Colt said, mouth grim, eyes hard.

"Sure it is. We're identical twins. Why is it so hard to see that I'm doing the same thing you did?"

"Exactly." Colt stomped across the room toward him and stopped. "Why can't you see it? Hell, maybe learn from my mistakes? You're doing the same damn thing I did, and I was wrong. If I remember right, it was you who called me an idiot over it."

Connor grimaced.

"Yeah. I ran from Penny. Doesn't make me proud to admit that. Makes me a damn coward."

"No, I was wrong back then. You were smart to trust your instincts."

Colt snorted a laugh. "If I'd done that, I would have stayed with her, because every instinct I had was telling me she was the real deal. The once in a lifetime. But I let my fear rule me. Just like you are."

Connor laughed and the sound scraped over his dry throat. He walked to the windows that overlooked the beach and the ocean below. The sun stained the morning sky rose and gold and there were whitecaps frothing on the water. Surfers were already out there, bobbing like corks in a bucket as they sat on their boards waiting for just the right wave. What should have been a soothing view did nothing to ease the knots inside him, though.

"I'm not afraid of anything." Then he heard Dina's voice in his head. *You're afraid, Connor. I know because I was scared, too.* Deliberately, he pushed it out.

"You think I don't know you?" Colt countered. "Think I can't see it? You're quaking in your boots, man."

"Go away."

Colt snorted. "No. I'm gonna save you from yourself."

"Just butt out, Colt. Do us both a favor."

"You can try to blow this off, but it's not working."

Colt walked up and stood beside his brother, both of them looking out over the water. "I tried the same damn thing. Told myself Penny was just in it to use me. Thought she wanted money, or whatever, but all she wanted was *me*." He shook his head slowly as if he still could hardly believe his good fortune.

"No accounting for taste," Connor mused, and felt the knots inside him tighten.

"Right," Colt said, nodding sagely. "Easier to make jokes than to face what's right in front of you. I tried that, too. Didn't work for me, either."

Con remembered what Colt had gone through when he and Penny were trying to work out what had brought them together. He remembered finding it damned amusing too. Wasn't so funny when he was in the hot seat. "John Ballas grabbed Dina at the party last night."

Colt stiffened instantly. "Bastard. Tried that with Penny, too. She dumped her drink on his head. The man thinks he can get away with anything."

"Yeah, well, we're done with him. I don't care how much business we lose."

"Agreed. How'd Dina handle him?"

Connor shoved his hands into his slacks pockets and fisted them there where his brother couldn't see them. "She didn't. I saw them moving off toward the bushes and I intercepted them. Tossed Ballas aside."

"Good for you. Wish I'd had the chance."

"Then later," Connor added, "I accused Dina of cheating on me with him." God, just saying the words out loud shamed him. He knew damn well what John Ballas was like. Hell, he knew Dina wasn't cheating. His *wife* had been accosted and he'd turned on *her*.

Stunned, Colt stared at him, openmouthed. "Are you out of your mind?"

"I don't know," Connor admitted. "Maybe."

A low whistle slipped from Colt. "No wonder Dina was so mad this morning."

"That wasn't the only reason."

"Connor…"

"You know what?" He glanced at his twin. "I don't need to hear any more from you."

Colt studied him. "No, you need to hear it from Dina. But that's gonna be tough, since she's gone."

"Gone?" His heart stopped. Hell, a part of him felt like the *world* had stopped. "What do you mean gone?"

"What do you think it means? She left. She told Penny this morning that she was leaving."

"And you didn't mention it until *now*?" Connor turned and headed for the door.

"I wanted to hear your side and now that I have, I don't blame her."

"Thanks for the support."

"When you do something right, I'll support you. In this?" Colt shook his head. "You're on your own."

On his own. It was the way he'd lived his entire adult life, Connor thought as he left the office, his brother's words still ringing in his ears. Connor had never let anyone close—at least, no one outside the family—except Jackie and even she had turned on him, so didn't that justify his actions now? Didn't that explain why the hell he'd snapped? Didn't that prove him right to be suspicious of everyone?

But those suspicions had brought him here. In the car, heading south, Connor fought down the panic that began to race through him. It didn't matter what she'd told Penny. Dina wouldn't leave. She'd stay and fight through this. He thought of all the times she had gone toe to toe with him, standing her ground, arguing her position and not giving way even when he tried to throw his weight around.

He kept telling himself that she was too stubborn, too unwilling to give an inch to ever run from an argument. But then he remembered the look on her face the night before. The touch of her hand on his cheek and the regret in her eyes when he tossed her confession of love back at her.

He slammed the heel of his hand against the steering wheel and flipped the visor down to block the morning sunlight. If she had left, he'd just follow her and get this settled, one way or another. If she had left, he told himself, he'd find her at her bungalow. He knew she'd kept it, so where else would she run?

Settle it. How would he settle it? Could he let go of years of self-protection and let himself trust a woman? If he couldn't, was he really willing to lose Dina?

No. That he wouldn't do. Just the thought of never seeing her again made his breath lock in his chest. What was it Colt had said? That he'd known Penny was the once-in-a-lifetime woman.

Well, for Connor, Dina was that woman. That one in a million he hadn't believed existed. The woman he'd been too stupid to appreciate until it was too late. No. It wasn't too late. He'd figure this out. Despite what his brother might think, Connor was a smart guy. There was an answer. He just had to find it.

At his house, he parked, jumped out of the car and hit the front door running. He took the stairs two at a time, his own footsteps thundering through the quiet house.

Too quiet, his mind warned. The kids should be up and playing, squealing. There should be the scent of scrambled eggs and coffee in the air, but there was nothing.

The house, like Connor, felt abandoned.

At the landing, he walked down the hall, turned into the triplets' suite and stopped dead. The beautiful room was empty. He forced himself over the threshold and looked around, as if he were expecting to find the kids and Dina hiding behind the furniture. But there was no one and his footsteps echoed eerily in the quiet.

His gaze swept the completed room. Rafe had outdone himself. The suite was huge, with a bay window complete with child safety rails and a bathroom designed for small children, with counters and even the tub shorter than normal. There were three matching white cribs that would become daybeds as the kids grew and bookshelves filled with storybooks and toys. Dressers in a walk-in closet held their clothes and soft rugs covered the wood floor. The walls were dotted with framed images from children's stories along with pictures of family.

Almost without knowing where he was headed, Connor moved to the photo of Jackie and Elena. He met his old friend's eyes and felt the anger finally fade. She'd hurt him. Lied to him. But because of her and Elena, he had the triplets in his life. And up until last night, he'd had Dina.

Now all he had to do was get her back.

He ran out of the room, down the stairs and skidded to a stop before slamming into his housekeeper. "Louise. When did they leave?"

The older woman frowned at him, folded her arms over her chest and tapped the toe of one sturdy black shoe against the floor. She sniffed. "Before breakfast. They were crying. *All* of them."

He caught the glimmer of tears in Louise's eyes as well and guilt took a bite out of him, but he swallowed down the pain.

"I'm going to get them now," he told her and started for the door.

"You'd better bring Dina and those children home where they belong," she called out and had him stopping in surprise.

When he looked back at her, she hadn't changed position but managed to look even more disappointed in him.

"Until they come home, I'm on strike. You can cook and clean for yourself, Connor King."

"You can't go on strike," he argued.

"Watch me," she said shortly, then whirled around and quick marched down the hall to the kitchen.

Yeah, looked like he had a *lot* of things to straighten out.

Dina was done crying.

She hadn't slept the night before and most of today had been spent soothing the triplets, who were too young to know why their daddy wasn't with them. Thank heaven they were also too young to know what a jackass he was.

"You know you're welcome to stay with me as long as you like."

"Thank you, Abuela," Dina said and curled her feet up under her on her grandmother's couch. "But I'll start looking for a place for the four of us tomorrow."

She sent a look at the three babies on her grandmother's living room floor. Hopefully, they would get accustomed quickly to not having Connor around all the time.

"You're not going back to the bungalow?"

"It's too small," she said. And crowded with memories. Connor had spent too much time there. She would see him in every room and be haunted by images of what might have been if he hadn't been so stupid.

"Ah. Well, if it is only size that concerns you, maybe you should go back to the home you left this morning."

Dina looked at her grandmother, surprised. "How can I go back there? After everything Connor said to me… no, I don't belong with him. Not anymore. And he doesn't want me, either."

"*Nieta*, you love the man."

"I'll get over it." In forty or fifty years.

"He loves you as well," her grandmother said and Dina laughed shortly. "I know what I saw. And on your wedding day, I saw a man in love."

"You're wrong." She wished her grandmother was right, but if she were, how could Connor have said all of those things to her?

"I am never wrong, *nieta*." A warm smile softened that statement. "You should know that by now."

"I'm sorry, Abuela," Dina said. "I know you mean well, but this is one story that won't have a happy ending. Even if Connor showed up right this minute and apologized, how could I ever forgive him for thinking so little of me?"

From her end of the couch, Angelica leaned forward, caught Dina's hand in hers and said, "For love, we do many things. We forgive thoughtlessness, carelessly given pain and the mistakes that all people make. And you must take pity on a man as well," her grandmother added, sitting back again. "They do not adapt to deep emotions as well as women do. They fight against love as if feeling deeply somehow weakens them." She shrugged. "They're foolish, because loving makes you strong. Strong enough even to forgive."

Dina watched her grandmother and wished she were half as nice a person as Angelica Cortez. She didn't know if she would be able to forgive Connor, but thought it probably didn't matter since he would never come around to apologize. When the doorbell rang, the older woman said, "Ah. It is time."

Suspicion awakened inside Dina. "Time for what?"

Her grandmother smiled and walked to answer the door. "Time to see how strong your love is, *nieta*."

"Is she here?"

Connor's voice pulled Dina to her feet. Her heart leapt, her stomach did a quick tumble, but she was standing when he rushed into the living room, followed more slowly by her grandmother. "Traitor," she murmured.

"I love you as well," Angelica said with a smile. Then she added, "I will be in the kitchen making some tea."

Connor didn't hear her leave. He hardly saw the elegant older woman. All he could see was Dina. All he was aware of was that his heart was beating again. He hadn't been sure it ever would when he drove to Dina's old bungalow and found it as empty as his own house was.

That's when he remembered her grandmother. One call to the older woman had assured him that Dina and the kids were safe, and as Angelica had told him, the rest was up to him.

"Dina—"

"Da!" Sam called out and then all three of the babies were hurrying toward him and greeting him as if he'd been gone a year. And really, that's what it felt like. He hugged, he kissed, he patted and when the trips had gone back to playing, he stood up and faced the woman watching him through dark eyes shadowed with wary caution.

He couldn't blame her.

"Connor, I don't want to talk to you anymore."

"You don't have to," he said, taking a half step toward her. "Just listen. *Please.*"

She took a deep breath and then slowly nodded.

His gaze locked on her, Connor felt his world fall back into place. She stood in a slant of sunlight that shone in her hair and sparked in her eyes. Her features were closed, but she wasn't throwing him out, so he called that a win. He had one chance to make this count. To convince her that she was the most important thing in his life.

"Everything I said last night was wrong," he blurted and watched surprise flicker in her eyes. "I didn't even believe it when I was saying it. Oh, and as for John Ballas, he's done. We're through working with him and if I ever see him again, I'll punch him just for the hell of it."

She laughed a little at the image and he smiled too before he said, "The truth is, Dina, I'm out of my depth here. I didn't expect you. Didn't expect to *care* for you—"

"I know that," she said softly. "You made it clear when we got married that you weren't looking for a wife so much as a bed partner and a mom for the kids."

Connor winced and if he could have, he would have found a way to kick himself. "Yeah. I did. And I was wrong about that, too."

"Is that right?"

One corner of her mouth lifted briefly and Connor took that as a good sign. "I let my own past color how I treated you. In a way, I was holding you responsible for everyone who had ever tried to use me or my family."

"I wasn't—"

He held up one hand to stop her right there. "I know you weren't using me. I know you didn't lie or cheat or do any other damn thing wrong. That was all on me, Dina. I kept watching, waiting, sure that you'd betray me, and when you didn't, I panicked, because if you really were as wonderful as I thought, then I was in big trouble. Jackie was the last straw, you know? She was family and she turned on me and that hit me hard."

"Elena was my family and she lied to me about you, too," Dina pointed out.

"I know." He moved a little closer, sending a quick glance at the babies gathered on the floor. "And we let them get in the way. Me, more than you." Closer, one step, then another. She wasn't backing up. "Dina, when I went to the house and found it empty, something in me died. Without you and the kids there, it was emptier than anything I've ever known."

"I couldn't stay," she told him. "Not after last night."

"I know. I hurt you and I'm sorry. So damn sorry."

"Connor—"

"No," he interrupted quickly, feeling his heart begin to beat normally again at the shine in her eyes and the softening of her features. "Don't talk yet. Let me finish. Let me say that I do trust you, Dina. I want you to come home. I want all of us to live together. To build a real life."

She shook her head and he worried.

"Trusting me is good, Connor, but it's not enough," she said softly. "I told you last night that the reason I married you was because I love you. Well, I do. I love you so much that I can't live with you knowing you don't feel the same way."

A slow smile curved his mouth. "That's where *you're* wrong. I do love you, Dina. I love you more than I ever thought it possible to love anyone. You're the first thing I think of in the morning and the last thing I think of at night. I want to spend the rest of my life with you in my arms."

"You do?" Her mouth curved into a dreamy smile and Connor's heart filled.

"I do." Then he grinned. "It's like taking that vow all over again. I will love you forever, Dina. I want to take you and the kids home. I want us to build a life there. Have more babies there."

"God, Connor. I want to believe. I really do."

Dipping into his inside coat pocket, he pulled out a sheaf of papers and handed them to her. "I couldn't get here earlier today because I was at my lawyer's, having him draw up these papers for us."

She opened them, but frowned. "What is it?"

"It's the first of the steps we have to take to legally adopt the triplets."

She inhaled sharply. "Oh, Connor…"

He moved in closer and cupped her face in his palms. The warmth of her skin, the love in her eyes, chased away the last of the cold that had been smothering him since the night before. "We'll all be Kings, legally. We'll be a real family. We'll have each other. We'll have love. And if you can trust me, Dina, we'll be happy."

She stared into his eyes. "I didn't want to love you, Connor, because I was afraid that somehow I would lose myself in that love."

She went up on her toes and planted a quick kiss on his mouth, and that one small taste of her wasn't going to be nearly enough. But he kept quiet, needing to hear what she had to say, hoping it was what he needed to hear.

"But I'm not lost. I'm more found than I've ever been," she said, with a quick look at the babies, babbling and laughing. "You have my heart and I'm trusting you with it. Trusting you with all of our hearts."

The bands around his chest loosened and he drew his first easy breath in nearly twenty-four hours. Pulling her in close, he kissed her almost reverently. "I'll never let you down again, I swear it," he said. "And I will love you for the rest of my life and beyond."

"You'd better," she warned, then smiled as he bent his head to seal his promise with a kiss.

When they broke apart, he rested his forehead against hers. "Louise went on strike."

"What?" Her laugh made him feel warm right down to his bones.

"Yep. Threatened to make me eat my own cooking until I brought you and the kids home where you belong."

"Well," Dina said with a grin, "no wonder you hurried over here."

"Exactly," he said and kissed her again.

"This is wonderful."

They broke apart to look at Angelica as she walked into the room carrying a tray of cookies. Taking a seat on the couch, she set the tray onto the table and began dispensing cookies to the babies, who crowded eagerly around her.

"Now," the older woman said with a wink, "*nieta*, if your husband would bring in the tea and cups, we'll have a celebration before you all go home."

"Abuela," Connor said, bending to kiss the woman's cheek, "that's a great idea."

"We'll go together," Dina said, threading her fingers through his.

"Even better," Connor told her and kissed her again, knowing he was the luckiest man in the world.

* * * * *

And don't miss the next
BILLIONAIRES AND BABIES *story,*
WHAT THE PRINCE WANTS
from Jules Bennett.
Available June 2015!

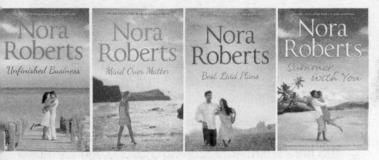
15_ST_11

MILLS & BOON®

The Thirty List

* cover in development

At thirty, Rachel has slid down every ladder she has ever climbed. Jobless, broke and ditched by her husband, she has to move in with grumpy Patrick and his four-year-old son.

Patrick is also getting divorced, so to cheer themselves up the two decide to draw up bucket lists. Soon they are learning to tango, abseiling, trying stand-up comedy and more. But, as she gets closer to Patrick, Rachel wonders if their relationship is too good to be true…

Order yours today at
www.millsandboon.co.uk/Thethirtylist